THAT OLD COUNTRY MUSIC

ALSO BY KEVIN BARRY

There Are Little Kingdoms

City of Bohane

Dark Lies the Island

Beatlebone

Night Boat to Tangier

THAT OLD COUNTRY MUSIC

Stories

KEVIN BARRY

DOUBLEDAY *New York*

This is a work of fiction. Names, characters, places, and incidents either are the product of the author's imagination or are used fictitiously. Any resemblance to actual persons, living or dead, events, or locales is entirely coincidental.

 Published in the United States by Doubleday, a division of Penguin Random House LLC, New York, and distributed in Canada by Penguin Random House Canada Limited, Toronto. Originally published in hardcover in Great Britain by Canongate Books Ltd., Edinburgh, in 2020.

www.doubleday.com

DOUBLEDAY and the portrayal of an anchor with a dolphin are registered trademarks of Penguin Random House LLC.

Several stories previously published in the following publications: *The Irish Times:* "Roethke in the Bughouse" (December 29, 2015) and "Who's-Dead McCarthy" (January 1, 2020); *The New Yorker:* "Ox Mountain Death Song" (October 22, 2012); "Deer Season" (October 3, 2016); and "The Coast of Leitrim" (October 8, 2018); "Toronto and the State of Grace" was originally collected in *Sex and Death: Stories,* edited by Sarah Hall and Peter Hobbs, published by Faber & Faber, Limited, London, in 2016.

Excerpt from *The Piano* © Jane Campion and Kate Pullinger, 1994, Bloomsbury Publishing Plc.

Book design by Anna B. Knighton
Jacket photographs: chair © conrado / Shutterstock;
painting © shutterupeire / Shutterstock; frame © worker/ Shutterstock;
landscape © Feifei Cui-Paoluzzo / Moment / Getty Images
Jacket design by Michael J. Windsor

Library of Congress Cataloging-in-Publication Data
Names: Barry, Kevin, 1969– author.
Title: That old country music : stories / Kevin Barry.
Description: First edition. | New York : Doubleday, 2021.
Identifiers: LCCN 2020012308 (print) | LCCN 2020012309 (ebook) |
ISBN 9780385540339 (hardcover) | ISBN 9780385540346 (ebook)
Classification: LCC PR6102.A7833 A6 2021 (print) |
LCC PR6102.A7833 (ebook) | DDC 823/.92—dc23
LC record available at https://lccn.loc.gov/2020012308
LC ebook record available at https://lccn.loc.gov/2020012309

MANUFACTURED IN THE UNITED STATES OF AMERICA

1 3 5 7 9 10 8 6 4 2

First United States Edition

For Lucy Luck and Declan Meade

I think that the romantic impulse is in all of us and that sometimes we live it for a short time, but it's not part of a sensible way of living. It's a heroic path and it generally ends dangerously. I treasure it in the sense that I believe it's a path of great courage. It can also be the path of the foolhardy and the compulsive.

—JANE CAMPION

Contents

The Coast of Leitrim / 1

Deer Season / 29

Ox Mountain Death Song / 47

Old Stock / 65

Saint Catherine of the Fields / 83

Toronto and the State of Grace / 99

Who's-Dead McCarthy / 117

Roma Kid / 131

Extremadura (Until Night Falls) / 153

That Old Country Music / 165

Roethke in the Bughouse / 179

THAT OLD COUNTRY MUSIC

THE COAST OF LEITRIM

LIVING ALONE in his dead uncle's cottage, and with the burden lately of wandering thoughts in the night, Seamus Ferris had fallen hard for a Polish girl who worked at a café down in Carrick. He had himself almost convinced that the situation had the dimensions of a love affair, though in fact he'd exchanged no more than a few dozen words with her, whenever she named the price for his flat white and scone, and he shyly paid it, offering a line or two himself on the busyness of the town or the fineness of the weather.

"It's like France," he said to her one sunny morning in June.

And it was true that the fields of the mountain had all the week idled in what seemed a Continental languor, and the lower hills east were a Provençal blue in the haze, and the lake when he lowered himself into it was so warm by the evening it didn't even make his midge bites sting.

"The heat," he tried again. "Makes the place seem like France. We wouldn't be used to it. Passing out from it. Ambulance on standby."

His words blurted at the burn of her brown-eyed stare. She didn't lose the run of herself by way of a response but she said yes, it is very hot, and he believed that something at least cousinly to a smile softened her mouth and moved across her eyes. He had learned already by listening in the café that her name was Katherine, which was not what you'd expect for a Polish woman but lovely.

At thirty-five years of age, Seamus Ferris was by no means setting the night on fire at the damp old pebbledash cottage on Dromord Hill, but he had no mortgage nor rent to pay, and there was money from when the father died, a bit more again when the mother went to join him, also the redundancy payment from Rel-Tech, and some dole. He had neither sister nor brother and was a little stunned at this relatively young age to find himself on a solo run through life. He had pulled back from his friends, too, which wasn't much of a job, for he had never had close ones. He had worked for eight years at Rel-Tech, but more and more he had found the banter of the other men there a trial, the endless football talk, the foolishness and bragging about drink and women, and in truth he was relieved when the chance of a redundancy came up. He had the misfortune in life to be fastidious and to own a delicacy of feeling. He drank wine rather than beer and favoured French films. Such an oddity this made him in the district that he might as well have had three heads up on Dromord Hill.

He believed that Katherine, too, had sensitivity. She had a dreamy, distracted air, and there was no question but that she seemed at a remove from the other mulluckers who worked in the café. The way she made the short walk home in the evenings to the apartments across the river in Cortober again named a sensitivity—she always slowed a little to look out and over the water, maybe to see what the weather was doing, perhaps she even read the river light, as Seamus did, fastidiously. He could keep track of her route home if he parked down by the boathouse, see the slender woman with brown hair slow and turn to look over the water, and it was only with a weight of reluctance that she moved on again for home.

In the sleepless nights of the early summer his mind ran dangerously across her contours. He played out many scenarios that might occur in the café, or around town, or maybe on a Sunday walk through the fields by the lake. It was a more than slightly different version of himself that acted his part in these happy scenes: Seamus as a confident and blithe man, but also warm and generous, and possessed of a bedroom manner suave enough to ensure that the previously reticent Polish girl concluded his reveries roaring the head off herself in gales of sexual transport. Each morning when he awoke once more in an aroused state—there was no mercy—it was of Katherine from the café that he thought. She was pretty but by no means a supermodel, not like some of the Eastern Europeans, with their cheekbones like blades, and as Seamus was not himself hideous, he felt he might have a chance in forgiving light. All he had to do was string out the few words right in his mouth.

He was in the café by now four or five times a week, and she was almost always on. The once or twice she hadn't been were occasions of crushing disappointment, and he'd glared hard at the mulluckers, as they bickered and barked like seals over the trays of buns and cakes. Even the hissing spout of the coffee machine was an intense annoyance when Katherine wasn't there. Along with its delicacy, Seamus's mind had, too, a criminal tendency—this is often the way—a kind of native sneakiness, though he would have been surprised to have been told this. The café's toilet was located right by the kitchen, and Seamus could not but notice what looked like a rota pinned to the back of the kitchen door. Catching his breath one Monday morning, he reached in with his phone and took a photograph, and in this way he had her hours for the week got. Also, her full name.

KATHERINE ZIELINSKI she was called, and he wasn't back in the van before he had it googled—it might be unusual enough inside quote marks to give quick results, and indeed within seconds he was poring over an Instagram account in her name. The lovely profile picture confirmed her identity—it was his Katherine all right, with her fourteen followers. She had posted only six times, six images, going back to the January previous, and relief flooded through him like an opiate when he found no photos of a boyfriend nor of a baby. It was something more intense than an opiate that went through him when he studied the most recent post, which was from the weekend just gone. It was of Katherine's right hand resting on the bare thighs revealed by her shortish denim skirt, and in the hand she clutched a slim box set—it was "Tales of the Four Seasons," four films by Éric Rohmer. Her accompanying caption read, "Goracy weekend."

It was a swift job to go to Google Translate with that and find that it meant, merely, "Hot weekend." She had humour as well as taste, it appeared, though in truth Seamie Ferris wouldn't be putting Rohmer at the top of the league in terms of the French directors; he would in fact rate him no more than highish in the second division, but at least he might be able to argue to her a rationale for this. Her knees were lovely and brown, though possibly a little thickset, but as it was a case of mother fist and her five daughters up in the pebbledash cottage, this was not a deal-breaker.

He spent time with the other images. He tried to decipher them or, more exactly, to decipher from them something of her character. Her only other personal appearance was in a blurry selfie that showed her reflection in a rain-spattered windowpane and that was suggestive, somehow, of Katherine as a solitary. There was a poor vista of the river from the bridge at evening. The rest of the images were reposted from other accounts—someone's pencil drawing of Sufjan Stevens; a cityscape that might have been of the Polish winter, its streetlights a cold amber; and, finally, a live shot of Beyoncé at a concert in Brazil in the stance of some new and utterly undefeatable sexual warrior. These images spoke to Seamus Ferris, in a low, insistent drone, of a yearning he recognised, and he felt that now he should end his playacting and confide his feelings to the woman.

The idea sent him into a foetal huddle on the couch, his back turned to the hot afternoon sun that poured through the window to show up the cottage in its bachelor meanness. The strangest thing he had learned while alone in his mid-thirties was about the length of the nights. They were never-fucking-ending. They opened out like bleak continents. They were landscapes sombre and with twisted figures. He lay there and flopped and muttered on the couch until the darkness again fell on Dromord Hill and the extent of the night shamelessly presented itself. He felt backed into a corner. He would have to ask her out. The worst that could happen was a refusal and the subsequent embarrassment of that, but there are worse things than embarrassment, he had learned, in the night, when his mind wandered across such things.

In the auditing of the night a plan had been laid down. He would raise the question on a Thursday morning, and so he had not shaved since the Monday—this provided a shadow of interest across what was in truth a weakish jawline. He scratched at the stubble helplessly as he picked at his scone, sipped at the cooling coffee.

His stomach tumbled and spoke. He would leave it until he was ready to depart, and if he was refused at least he would be out the door and could go and fuck himself into the Shannon. He was about to stand and make grimly for the counter—he felt like a man heading off to be shot—when she stepped out from behind it and for absolutely no good reason came to saunter around his table, looking out at the rain that as sure as Jesus had returned to make another wet joke of the summer.

"Back to the usual," she said.

"You'd nearly do away with yourself altogether," Seamus Ferris said.

"What do you mean?" she said.

"Nothing by it," he said. "Do you want to go out with me sometime?"

"That will be fine," she said. "When is this happening?"

HE BELIEVED NOW that they were in telepathic contact with each other. She must have known and read his intention. She must have known, too, that he had sensed her likely compliance. This was how fatedness worked, how love discovered itself. In the long three days, the endless three nights that led up to their Sunday meeting, he attempted to send mental messages down Dromord Hill and across the slow meander of the river. The content of these messages was even to himself uncertain but had to do with ardency and truth.

The Sunday of their arrangement came up to dense clouds and a heavy mugginess. He went to the toilet five times in the morning and took Imodium against the thunder of his insides. Attraction as physical catastrophe was not exactly news to Seamus Ferris. He had been besotted before. Always it was with slightly humourless-looking women who appeared to be in a condition of vague disbelief about the world. If involved in any level of romance, he was given to lurchy moves and hot declarations, and always in the past he had scared the women off within a few dates. He had not had anything even close to sex for three years. With his Katherine he vowed that all would be different.

He met her by the bridge at three—the arrangement was for a spin in the van.

"Have you ever been to the coast of Leitrim?" he asked her, unpromisingly.

"No," she said. "It has a coast?"

"The coast of Leitrim," he said, "is four kilometres long. Which is in fact the shortest length of coast belonging to any county in Ireland."

"Now I know," she said.

"I mean barring the landlocked counties," he said.

"Okay," she said.

As he drove and they went through the rituals of small talk, he tried to communicate with her directly, too, without words, by way of pure mental focus. He tried to let her know that he needed her badly and that in his own modest way he was a prospect. He told her that he had a house that wanted work but was situated well. There were few bills. There was more than an acre of land to grow vegetables and flowers, and already he had begun this garden. It could be beautiful yet, he said. As they drove out of the Cortober side of town, a parade of drunken women skittered towards the bridge in glittery cowboy hats and stretch-nylon skirts, with bottles of Skinny prosecco to hand and in their eyes the dissolute, the haunted look of a three-day hen at its fag end and emblazoned on their tight-fitting t-shirts the legend "MOHILL PUSSY POSSE," and with something already close to love he turned to see the tip of Katherine's nose rise to match his own disdain.

"Why would they do this to themselves?" Katherine said.

"There's a sickness around the place," Seamus said.

A rare thing occurred then in the van as it hoovered up the N4—a companionable silence. To his awe he found that they were perfectly comfortable with each other and they didn't even have to try.

THE COAST OF LEITRIM sat under a low rim of Atlantic cloud. The breeze made the cables above the bungalows whisper of the Sunday afternoon's melancholy. The waves made polite applause when they broke on the shingle beach. She told him that she came from Stalowa Wola, a small city in the south, and that she could not see herself going back there. His heart soared.

"Is there no work?" he said.

"Not much but it's not that. It's more that my family is there and that makes everything too . . ."

She struggled for the word.

"Close?" she tried.

"Clammy," Seamus said. "Families can be like that. Give a clammy feeling."

"Clammy?"

"Like a warm feeling but not in a good way," he said. "Sweat on your palms and at the base of your back. A nervous-type feeling."

"You're funny," she said.

"Thanks be to fuck for that," he said.

"But yes," she said. "Clammy."

They walked the shingle beach. He told her as much as was bearable to tell about himself. He had gone to college in Galway to study French and business, but he had not finished his degree. He was not by his nature a finisher of things, he said. He had never said this before or really even thought it and it was a surprise to him. It was all coming out before the soft lashes, the stare. He had worked for years in a factory, he said, and lived at home. (The way an eternity of cold dread could be packed into a single line.) Somehow he had not had the impulse to travel. He had not known what he was looking for, if anything at all, he said, until he turned from the bog road into the clearing on the wooded slope of Dromord Hill and found there the pebbledash cottage of the old uncle he had barely known, and he had recognised the place at once as his home.

"I would have been brought there as a child," he said. "I remember being taken up there after I made my Holy Communion. He gave me two sausage rolls for it."

"This is a custom?"

"No, usually people give you money, a tenner."

Their talk came in odd spurts and the trudge of their feet went slowly across the shingle but the ease they found outside and around the talk was soft magic. Here she is for me, he thought. Here is the woman at last that I can be alone with.

"I'd like to see it," she said.

"The which?" he said.

"The cottage," she said.

NO DOUBT it was national stereotyping to think so but she seemed to know her way around a head of cabbage. From his spice rack's broad selection she took some caraway seeds and softened them in hot, foaming butter and stir-fried shreds of the cabbage in the fat, and these were delicious with thick slices of bacon and the sourdough bread he had brought from the market. They ate in silence as the sun broke through to heat the last of the day and its warm light was lavish in the room. They kissed for a long while on the sofa and then went to bed and even that worked out well enough.

HE FELT HIMSELF FALLING. In the native way he was tormented now by his own happiness. He could not imagine a future day without Katherine. That would be hell. To be able to stand back from and recognise his obsession as exactly that did not lessen its extent nor remove its danger. He waited for her outside the café each day.

He kept step with her across the bridge to the Cortober side and together they slowed to look out over the water. Tears welled up in his eyes and he had to make out it was the breeze off the river was the cause of them.

"What is it?" she said. "Really?"

"I didn't realise I was so on my own," he said. "If we're going to be brutally fucken honest about things."

Typically in the evenings they drove up to the cottage. Its solitude in summer was bliss. His future plans spewed as they sat over a few glasses of wine. There was pale light until eleven o'clock still, the summer at its high pitch. They could back away from the town and the world altogether, he said. They could be next to self-sufficient on the mountain. The madness of what he was saying to a woman he'd been seeing for three weeks was evident even to himself and even as he said it, but she did not seem in any way put out. In fact, she asked serious questions about the land and the cottage, the drainage, and she did so with an air of owlish inquiry. Sniffily together they watched films by the Dardenne brothers (Belgians were allowed) and Julia Ducournau. On a clear night in mid-

July, he went outside very late—stepped softly so as not to wake her—to see the starlight fall on the mountain as she slept, and he made a ritual vow to remain true if not exactly to the reality of the small woman sleeping in his bed in the cottage then to the perfected version of her he had worked out in his scenarios, for he believed that this version could incorporate and sustain—that we must each of us dream our lovers into their existence.

And now the torment of his happiness was on his brow like bad fever.

And now the nights were not long enough.

BUT WHEN THEY SAT together on the sofa in the evenings he was inclined to reach across and drag the hem of her skirt back down over her knees. Prim, it must have seemed, and it became something like a nervous tic, something he had no control over. They were perfectly normal and functional knees, but somehow their slight thickness made them seem foreign to her otherwise slender legs. Protuberances, he came to think of them as. Those unfortunate protuberances. They started to play on Seamie Ferris's mind a bit. When he should have been thinking about other parts of her, he was thinking about her thickset fucken knees.

IN THE SORROW and remorse that mingled madly with his animal passion he spent a long time in the bed kissing her knees. He could not keep away from them in the dark. He cupped and whispered to them. He licked and stroked them. He spent serious time with them.

"Please," she said on a humid night in late July.

"What?" he said.

"Leave them," she said. "My knees."

"Why?"

"I fucking hate my knees," she said.

"Oh, my darling," he said.

"They're hideous," she said. "If I could cut the fucking things off me!"

"They're exquisite," Seamus Ferris said.

"You will get the scabs on your mouth for lies," she said.

"I have a dreadful fucken jawline," he said. "Weak, a weak jaw. Gives me an unreliable look. A chancer."

"But I like this little beard you have going on," she said.

SHE SPOKE hardly at all of home or family. Her name was really Katarzyna, she said, but since childhood she had preferred the English version—Poland was crawling with Katarzynas. The small extent of her belongings was sorrowful. They didn't take up a quarter of the space in the back of his van. He thought the heart was going to explode in his chest as he watched her shyly fold away her underwear in the drawer he had cleared for her. He came in close behind and kissed her neck. She sighed at his kiss as though in sadness but turned and held him and told him that she loved him, and Seamie Ferris was sucked through a hole in the universe.

ONE NIGHT, soon after she had moved in, he lay beside her in the darkness and watched her sleeping. She turned towards him in her sleep and she began to speak in Polish—a slow, anxious muttering, with the same words repeated over and over again, a phrase, almost musical, and eerie, a kind of narcotic intonation. Was it some old love that she pined for? Was there something more than her nature behind the air of distraction? How much had she not told him of her past?

The next night she rolled and turned again and repeated again in her sleep the same words and this time he took his phone up from the floor and recorded them.

He spent the best part of the next day roaming the wind-swayed fields of Google, searching out voice-recognition apps with translation modes, and eventually he found what was needed, uploaded his recording, and he had her night words got, or at least he had them got in a loose rendition.

A FEELING OCCURRED within Seamie Ferris sometimes as if a brim had been reached and now his own words must cascade and fountain. He confronted her in the kitchen. He was aware that he had a face on him like his father's. Untrusting and cold.

"You've been talking in your sleep," he said.

"What do you mean?"

"You've been saying things, and it seemed to me it was the same thing, over and over, and I couldn't help but . . ."

"If only you could sleep," she said.

"I couldn't help but record it."

"You . . ."

"With the phone. I know, yeah. And I had it translated."

"By who?"

"By an app."

"What have I been saying?"

"That you'll die if ever I leave you."

"Oh Jesus God." She held her face in embarrassment.

"At least I think you're talking about me," he said.

"Who else would I be talking about?" she said.

SEAMUS FERRIS could bear a lot. In fact, already in his life he had borne plenty. He could handle just about anything, he felt, shy of a happy outcome. As the summer aged he became unseated by her trust of him and by her apparent want for him. What kind of a maniac could fall for the likes of me, he wondered. The question was unanswerable and terrifying. When she lay in his arms after they had made love, his breath caught jaggedly in his throat and he felt as if he might choke. To experience a feeling as deep as this raised only the spectre of losing it. As she lay sleeping in the night his mind now began to work up new scenarios. These played out variations around a single narrative line—the way that it would all cave in, the way that it would end, the way that he would be crushed beneath the rubble of his broken heart. Katherine coughing blood in the sink one morning, and then the quick raging of her demise—an illness like a wild animal tearing through her—and the way she would die a bag of bones in his arms. Jesus Christ. Or . . . Katherine leaving without a word, absconding on the Dublin train from Carrick station, returning to Poland and the lumpen embrace of some previous, unnamed love, some steelworker fucker with a head on him like a thirty-kilo kettlebell. Or . . . Katherine stumbled upon in a dark corner of a late-autumn field, at evening, blowing a young farmer. Or . . . an old farmer. So rancid did his night scenarios become that Seamie Ferris stumbled from the bed to the bathroom and gargled with Listerine. In the morning, still sleepless, he watched her carefully over their yogurt and fruit.

"They say you can tell by the chin," he said.

"What do you mean?"

"You know full well, I'd say. The way a liar can be made out by the set of the chin."

"Seamus?"

"Shay-moos," he mimicked. "Who were you with before me?"

"This is ridiculous. Why are you so jealous?"

"Because you have me fucken destroyed," he said. "I'm very sorry, Katherine. I just don't know that I'm fit for you."

"Ah, please," she said.

"Or for anybody," he said, and he stood up and walked out of the house.

THE SUMMER gave way without complaint. The light was thickening over the river now before eight. The long draw was well advanced. On Dromord Hill the colours of heartbreak came through. She had left him at the end of August. She moved back to the same apartment complex on the Cortober side. For almost the whole month of September Seamie Ferris slept like the dead. He would be up out of the bed for no more than an hour at a time, often much less. He had refused happiness when it was presented to him in the haughty form that he had always craved. What kind of a fucken fool was he? He drank milk from the carton by the light of the fridge in the middle of the night—never before in his life had he drunk from the lip of the carton. His skin itched and he had a whistling pain out the left lung. He believed that he might die. The two of them together could have made a small aloof republic on Dromord Hill—they could have written the rules for it. October. November. He hardly saw the town. He shopped at the Lidl on the Cortober side when he knew she'd be at work. On a dank winter morning he was trying to retrieve his coin from the trolley when a mullucker from the café came by, her face softening at the sorrowful sight of him.

"Did you hear at all?" she said, twisting the knife. "Did you hear Katherine went back?"

BUT NOW out of the winter-grey sky the soft magic again descended and he knew that the extent of his feeling was beyond the ordinary realm. He came to believe again that they were in telepathic contact with each other. Distance was no object to it. He sent mental messages down Dromord Hill and across the midland plain and across all the seas and the cities until at last the city of Stalowa Wola presented itself. The message he received back was that he must come to her and quickly.

He flew on a Ryanair to Wrocław and took a bus, a train, and then another bus until he found the place. It was a new-looking city with vast white fields opening everywhere in the distance. He walked the freezing afternoon away. He had no idea how to find her. He had to trust that he would be steered. There was a Tesco on the outskirts that made the place oddly familiar. He might well be mad, but what of it? He must find her.

An icy rain came across his face as he walked on. In an empty bar in what appeared to be the centre of the city, he drank a glass of red wine and tapped into his phone the wifi code. He went to the first place he always went—her Instagram account. It was fourteen minutes since she had at last posted a seventh image. It showed a detail of Dromord Hill—a whitethorn bank—in an evening sun flare. Her accompanying caption read, *"Mam na mysli lato."*

Google Translate: "I am thinking of summer."

Beneath her profile on the post was the place from which it had been sent—Kafé Komputery. He showed this name to the barman, and was directed to it. It was two lefts and a right, a five-minute walk. It must have been the last internet café in Europe. Its dim lights were cinema against the falling dark. Katherine, paler, still lovely, was at a terminal—all the others were unoccupied.

She turned at once at the scraping of the door as he entered.

"Oh, thanks be to fuck," she said.

DEER SEASON

SHE SAW HIM often in the morning and often again around dusk as he walked out by the river. She called him the riverman. She had seen him only in the distance and had not properly distinguished his features. She was almost eighteen and determined to have a fuck before it, but she lived remotely and the summer was almost over. He was tall and thin and did not have a pronouncedly masculine walk—he could not be taken for a farmer. His step was carefully picked out and it had a hesitancy to it. He brought to her mind the heron. She needed to get closer to him quickly.

The morning was bright, with a breeze that moved the light's sharp points on the lanes, and the hedges were opulent with berries and the high grasses raced in the late-summer fields. She set out for the banks of the river along the lit points of the lanes. She had taken a book for cover, after a long think about which book exactly to take. She pulled her cardigan tight against the morning chill that marked the season's changing. Even before the river's sour waft was in her nose, she had decided on the tree that she would sit beneath. She arranged the picture in her mind. She felt that she could see what was coming and that she could make events turn to her design. She felt a quick thrum of new sexual power. She fretted that the cardigan—a grey—might seem a little nunly, but if nunly, she reasoned, perhaps an intriguing counterpoint to the somewhat lurid cover of the Bolaño novel, which showed a Mexican death's head. Often her thoughts went in these contrary directions at once. He might not be a reader at all. He might be curt and indifferent to her, but this was not what she made out from the hesitant, loping step. She would bet the farm on manners.

The country was beautiful now that August was almost over. The heavier growth was done with and the tall grasses that moved in the breeze had faded to a whitish gold, and the reed banks were a still paler gold, and the yellow flags of June had withered on the long stems but moved in their flayed tatters yet—she endured rather than enjoyed all this. She had declared herself a Romantic, and bare winter was her idyll. There was a chill from the river and fingers of mist crept from it and a dampness rose into her from the shaded ground she sat on beneath the tree.

She opened the book and set it on her thighs and tried to read about strangulated prostitutes in the desert, but the words swam madly. She was very nervous. He showed soon enough around the bend of the river and she drew him towards her along the line. She saw now as he came closer that he was in fact much older than her, maybe in his thirties, and she knew that he registered her.

"I'm ready," she said, under her breath, and he stopped in his tracks and waved; he came still closer.

She saw at near range that he was good-looking enough, with a long and sharp-featured face that was pinched with kindness, and scruffy hair with some grey in its wires, and his eyelashes closed slowly now and opened again, a long exposure to inspect her.

"Hello," he said.

"Hi."

Their words were incongruous on the air. The moment of the riverbank here was seldom touched by human voices, but now it held clearly the riverman's and the girl's, and they both smiled at the fact of their intrusion on this place. There was only, as it got up again, the breeze among the grasses to distract them from each other, and they both looked out and across the moving grasses, as though casually, as though on the off chance of news. He turned back to her again with the knit bones of his smile. The smile was like something he had trapped, she thought.

"I think I've seen you before," he said.

This was a revelation, and it needed to be answered inside the beat of a second. If he had seen her loitering in the fields, he might have seen the way that she watched him, too, and read her intention, and despite all that she had drilled into herself about not appearing eager she fixed her hair now with her fingertips, and even before the strand of hair was settled behind her ear she cursed silently the obviousness of the gesture. He got down on his haunches, laid a hand to his long, skinny knee, and smiled at her; she set the book to one side.

"I live over that way," she said.

"Ah, yeah," he said, and he twisted his face to read the name on the book's cover.

"Roberto . . ."

"Bolaño," she said.

"Any good?"

"He's dead."

"Oh. That's gloomy."

"No, it isn't. I mean . . . the book isn't."

She had worried that the book might be a terrible idea, but here it was, doing its work, opening a pathway to conversation. She didn't have any great desire for the man, but she liked his voice, and he wasn't fat—he definitely didn't sound as if he came from around here; he was English, but country English. He wanted the talk to continue—she could see that well enough.

"I had to burn half my books last year," he said. "I had a very bad chest cold and I couldn't get out and all my fuel was gone."

Now she recognised the hesitancy of his walk for what it was, for poverty. He had the hunted look of rural poverty. His clothes were not good—army surplus, with ugly stout boots—but his limbs were long and lean and she was inclined to keep the conversation going; in just a week she would be eighteen.

"So cold you had to burn books?"

"Remember the cold snap, January? It was evil around here."

"I'd have been away," she said. "School."

"School still?"

"For another year," she said, and let a slyness assert. "Where do you go in the mornings?"

"I go up the Forestry," he said. "Though I shouldn't tell."

"Why not?"

"I've been taking some wood down. I'm leaving it to dry out. September, I'll start lugging it back to my place. You know they say it warms you three times, wood. When you cut it down, when you carry it, when you burn it."

"You're thinking ahead."

"That's right."

"And you're stealing from the Forestry."

"They've plenty."

"What if you were caught?"

"You'd need to be pretty stupid to be caught. It's vast, the Forestry. It goes right from here? Right from here and over the Ox Mountains."

"What's your name?"

"I'm Edward."

"I think you're a strange fish, Eddie."

"A cold fish was what I was, last winter. And I'm definitely not an Eddie. What's your name?"

THE NEXT DAY they met not quite by arrangement but by understanding. This time he sat beside her under the tree. She was very tense, though she pretended not to be as she sat with her legs kicked out in front of her; she was without the pretence of a book this time. Their bodies were tight and agitated in this proximity, but each face was half turned for its glance to lock on the other's. Sentimental grasses wavered in a lighter breeze. Autumn was moving in with stealth—early in the morning there had been stags' roars beyond the trees. He asked about her life, and she sighed impatiently and ticked off the father and the farm, the dead mother, the older brother, William, who was away to be a doctor, the significant fact of her return soon to boarding school, and she was aware that every word signified the extent of the gap between them, in this country, at this time, and the gap would, of course, feed into his fantasies about her, which she was sure were already hot, foetid, and possessing, and now the four days until the train went back through the Midlands to her school seemed like all the time in the world to make this happen. She decided that she found him attractive enough for the job at hand. She touched him for the first time, just the pads of her fingertips to his skinny biceps—like a dog's muscle, it twitched madly—and he rose, half terrified, his neck a rush of crimson, and made off down the river. She would need to be gentle with him.

"Enjoy the timbering," she called, and she may have accentuated the switching of her hips as she moved off and away from the river herself, across the pale-gold fields; he would crane for as long as he could to follow her walk, she was sure of that, until she had disappeared from view, and he would be away to masturbate immediately in the woods then—she was sure of that, too. It was as easy as making a ladybird walk up the stem of a leaf.

That night brought a warm heavy rain that told the last heat of the year was on the way, and Thursday came up to the promised heat. She wore a skirt and applied some colour to her lips. Her father watched her as if it were a painted fox that crossed his yard. The morning was swampish and there was a rotten-vegetable stink from the ditches and the berries were dull jewels on the hedges—she wanted it to happen quickly and then to be done with the whole unfathomable business. Her lips moved, she made words on the air as she walked, saying lowly, and determinedly, "I will make . . . of this riverbank . . . a fuckery."

And a bead of desperation formed in the indent above the centre of her lips. She was in a condition, all the same, of vaulting readiness. The bones of her feet beat down the path to the river and there, already, the riverman was waiting. He had a face on him like a washed dog. He was quieter, shyer, and even more awkward this hot morning, knowing as well himself that the moment had arrived, even before she turned to him, midway through a ridiculous halting conversation about dragonflies peculiar to the vicinity, and kissed him so hard and viciously she might have drawn blood. They rose then from beneath the tree and went away into the reeds like animals of the place.

She lay down on the ground and he lay down on top of her and kissed her and moved against her for a short while and then went further and there was hardly any of the supposed pain and really to the girl it just seemed badly designed, fiddly, a contrivance, a make-do job (as her father might say), and he rolled off her just in time and rose onto his knees and came on the ground. A little boy's remorse filled up his eyes.

"Is that about the size of it?" she said.

"Yeah," he said.

There was nowhere left for them to go but into their own breathing flesh again, now that they were so quickly separated.

HE DIDN'T SHOW UP by the river the following day or the next, and so on the evening before her departure she set out to find his house. She knocked on his door and let the raps play out a jaunty, half-comical rhythm.

"Oh sweet Jesus fuck," he said when he opened the door, and sharply he hustled her inside.

The house was a small bungalow—it was clean and tidy and reeked of animal want. He kept his back turned to her as he filled the kettle and set it to boil. Misery was essayed everywhere, in the lentils soaking on the draining board, in the way that he tried to scour a tea mug with his index finger under the running tap—she saw his glum and mortified face in the dulling window; the evening was already fading outside, late August leaning into September.

"It's the sort of thing that could get me in a lot of trouble around here," he said.

"Who'll know?" she said.

He sucked his teeth and rolled a cigarette with the long, slightly crooked fingers that were the most elegant thing about him and lit the cigarette and puffed out the smoke nervously.

"You are seventeen?" he said.

"Not for long," she said.

"I don't need a friend," he said.

"And I no more want tea than the fucken wall," she said.

When they had finished, this second and final time, and while he dozed or pretended to in the bedroom, she went through the narrow hallway and into the kitchen again; she examined his lair. There was a library book about foraging. There was the disheartening musk of adult maleness. There was a book about the bogs. There was *The Sorrows of Young Werther*—she had known well enough what she was doing. There was something military about the neatness. She stood in the doorway and envisioned his many possible lives and looked out to the blue night falling. Across the fields, she could hear the river moving. The river talked to itself of all that it had seen. She stood there for some time, until the blue had thickened to near-blackness, and she entered a spell of heavy dreaming or quietude such as can open out sometimes in youth if the person is to be an artist, and now the stars came through, and when she heard his wordless shuffling behind her to break the spell she walked away through the yard and did not once look back.

HALF A TERM PASSED in the ritual frenzies of gossip and competition. She embellished gladly as she confided her late-summer adventure. She told her friends that he had looked a bit like a skinnier Rufus Wainwright and was nearly as camp. Her father made his usual Sunday night phone calls and was full of his usual quiet news, mostly about deer and his son—Oh, Willie was home the weekend, we went out; Willie got a buck, I got nothin'—but then the third week of October her father did not make his call. It was the first time ever that he had missed the call, and she knew at once why—he had got word of her adventure. She knew on the train home for midterm break that the great scene awaited but, still, to hear her father use the words he did was astonishing.

"What would your dead mother say if she knew I'd raised up a slut?"

"Where the fuck am I supposed to go with a question like that?"

"And the tongue on it!"

The quasi-biblical phrasing that had lurched in—raised up? In what demented reach of his person had he been storing this language? The late October day was peeled and cool; the light was miserly by six, the last remnants clawed in weak scratches across the sky. She stood with her back to the piano. The room was dense with gloom. The important news was that he was gone.

"He was ran out of it," her father said.

"He was ran where?"

"He was ran!"

"Who ran him?"

Her father reddened dangerously and made to cross the floor but caught himself and turned his back to her. He spoke to the wall.

"Did you protect yourself?"

"Ah, here," she said.

"Did you not think it through?"

"I did not."

"Did you protect yourself?"

"Nothing happened, Da."

"You were seen!"

"By fucken who! Are they hangin' out of the fucken trees?"

He turned and again made to cross the floor to her, but, once more, he caught himself.

"Where'd he go to, Da?"

"How'd I know that? Jesus Christ, girl! I mean any young fella at all your own age and I'd nearly understand it. The halfwit eejit of the Creminses even. But this aul' English hoor? You know he's astray in the head, you do? You know he's been in and out of the hospital? Ten months in that place below and he paid rent twice."

"How was he ran, Da?"

"We were respectable people! At one time. Around here. You know that, don't you?"

"Was he hurt, Daddy?"

The lurch of fright in her voice was a sickening thing and she fled the room in disgust at it. The fright betrayed a weight of feeling that was a surprise to her. She had carried it without knowing. Though she knew well enough that it was the idea of him rather than the fact—the idea of a long, thin, sombre man, in a soak of noble depression, smelling of lentils, in a damp pebbledash bungalow, amid a scrabble of the whitethorn trees, a man ragged in the province of Connacht and alone at all seasons, perhaps already betrothed to a glamorous early death, and under some especially mischievous arrayment of the stars he was all that a girl could ask for.

THERE WOULD HAVE BEEN no gothic scene. There would have been no baying mob. There would have been a rapping on the door one evening of the autumn, and quiet words spoken, and their intent understood at once. He would have packed his few things in a holdall and the next morning taken the bus from Ballymote.

He would cross the country and the sea again. He would settle in a city of the north and try to find work and fail, and try to find a hostel and fail, and seek again the needle's tip and solace. On the needle's tip he would nod and dream of the Forestry land rising up to the Ox Mountains and the slight girl with dyed black hair on the riverbank there one morning.

SHE CROSSED THE FIELDS again as the October dark fell. She walked now beneath a cloak of widowly despair. She had arranged the picture for this scene, too. She came on his bungalow in full darkness. It had not been let again, and the door was unlocked. All had been packed away and swept neatly. His bedroom was bare, the kitchen so bare. She sat on the kitchen floor long into the night. Outside, late on, something thrashed through the whitethorn and the sally trees. She knew it was a deer, and a young one by the measure of fright in its movement. But the night folded again into the quiet of its soft enclosure. It was moonless and the great dark pressed in. She reached out for him in the dark. When she at last rose to go she was stiff from the cold and felt many years older as she left the house and made for home through the night and dark and the pads of her feet beat out the new soft rhythm of her power.

OX MOUNTAIN DEATH SONG

- 1 -

HE HAD BEEN PLANTING babies all over the Ox Mountains since he was seventeen years old. Well, he had the hair for it, and the ferret grin, and there was hardly a female specimen along that part of the Sligo–Mayo border that hadn't taken the scan of his hazel glance, or hadn't had the hard word laid on, in the dark corners of bars, or in the hormone maelstrom of the country discos, or in untaxed cars, down backroads, under the silly, silly moonlight. He had soft girlish eyelashes and pig-ignorant shoulders—sex on a stick, was his own opinion, and too many of the girls, too many of the women, shared it. He kept several on the string at any given time but as soon as they got weight on them he left them.

Now there are those who in a lifetime cannot leave a woman—who cannot gather the strength or get past the sentiment—but Canavan left them every day.

- 2 -

THE FIRST TIME Sergeant Brown came across this latest Canavan—he was from a family a long while notorious—was in the station house, when the boy was fourteen, and had totalled a stolen Celica on the Ballymote road, and the first thing the sergeant did was hit him the slap of a phone book across the back of the head.

"That'll take the fucken ferret out of you," he said, though of course it did not, and Canavan just smirked, sexily.

The witch hazel of the eyes and the sulphur of the smirk—these betrayed to the sergeant that young Canavan would at some future point kill.

He hit him another slap of the phone book.

"Lose the fucken face!" he cried. "You're nothin' only a fucken knacker off the Ox!"

If the regal youth felt pain it did not show. He merely flicked his blond fringe, spat a tooth, and spoke in a voice already deep-down and mannish.

"And you're nothin' only a fucken swing-key," he said.

- 3 -

COME UP TO a humid Sunday of late June—

The day had the ominous feeling of such grey dense Sundays—it was sour with foreboding—as the vapours of paranoia floated in from Killala Bay, and the ridgeback line of the Ox Mountains lay prone, like a crouched beast, their tone dark bluish in the haze, sombre, and watchful like a beast.

The detective, Sergeant Brown—Sergeant Tom Brown,

plainly—drove an unmarked Primera along the sea road in his flop sweat and rancour.

"Bastard," he said.

He was trying to keep a fix on the Canavan's movements but it was to no avail—the fucker was like water through your hands. And what troubled the sergeant above all was the fact of the fungating mass. This Canavan was not long for the world or its women.

He might do anything now.

- 4 -

SERGEANT BROWN was from a line of guards. His father had been the sergeant at Aughris before he drank himself into the clay of the place. His father's father had at the time that it was still Royal Irish Constabulary been the sergeant at Ballincarrow before he drank himself into the clay of the place. His father's father's father had been the sergeant at Easkey when they were still jawing grass at the side of the road and spitting the green juice, and he, too, had drank himself into the clay of the place.

Sergeant Tom Brown did not drink. He suffered instead the terrible want of a sweet tooth. Sugar ran him. He sat in a humid murk, himself vaporous, gently steaming, in the Primera, outside the Emo station, on the N59, beneath the hateful shadow of the Ox, and he ate a Swiss roll.

He looked at himself in the mirror—the big sticky face on it like a child's.

"Here's another day I get fucken fatter," he said.

He wheezed terribly now climbing a stair. He wheezed as hard again coming down. He hadn't enjoyed a mirror since the late eighties. He was sixty-five now and just three weeks from his retirement—his determination was to have Canavan looked after before it.

- 5 -

THE CONSULTANT ONCOLOGIST at the Regional Hospital went back so far with the sergeant that they had done the long jump together. He was not only his oldest but among his most useful confidants. Canavan's tumour, he explained, was feeding on his very youth and vitality.

"An auld fella might slow it," he said. "A young fella won't."

It was pacing hard. It was spreading all over. It had gone into the lymph. Canavan, in his manly noon, at twenty-nine years of age, had refused the treatment, having been told it would likely make him impotent and the hair fall out.

"He won't see Christmas lights, Tom," the oncologist said.

And they both knew what that meant.

Canavan could do anything now.

- 6 -

HE WAS ABOUT the Ox country yet. This much the sergeant knew for sure. And about the Ox his powers were affiliated with the supernatural—you could corner him to a patch of ground the width of a postage stamp but even so he would wriggle free, and have time enough to look back over the shoulder, lock a glance, and smoulder.

He knew the bog roads, the copses, the cypress arbours. He knew the recesses of the hills and the turlough hides. He knew the crannies of the coast. He knew the new-build estates and the spread and bungalow drift of the ever-changing villages, and the backways of townlands, and the gardens of priests, and the old walled demesnes, just as he knew the lairs of ripe widows, and the dampish, seablown, lavatorial odour of beachside apartments, and knew the tin-roofed sheds, the outbuildings, the caves. He knew Zion Hill and the Union Wood. He knew the ruts and tunnels of the country, the country of the Ox, a post-glaciated terrain, and knew where mountains had moved, the cracks and openings that were made—he knew the country of the Ox, and the infinite thousands of its hiding places.

\- 7 -

A CANAVAN KNEW also the greatest of the male consolations—that a girl could be made to laugh, a girl with an apple-cheeked arse. The pale-green days of these Atlantic reaches could be enlivened only by fucking and fighting—moments of violent glow—and the Canavan magic was to make sparks from little. Each in the stepped line of the generations was a taunt to the next: a taunt to exceed, go further. Everything was passed down, the gestures even. The curl of lip and set of shoulders, and the weird skills, too, as in the way a Canavan could by wary nature catch on the air the tang of policeman—to a Canavan, it had an aniseed note.

The years gave in, the years gave out, and only the trousers changed—breeches of sackcloth gave way to rain-soaked gabardine, gave way to tobacco-scented twill, and on to the denim variations (boot cut; straight leg; at glamorous times, beflared) and then to the nylon track-pant, and then to the cotton sweats. The signal gesture of a Canavan in all this time did not change: it was a jerk of thumb to the waistband to hoick up the pants.

The Canavans—they had for decades and centuries brought to the Ox elements that were by turn very complicated and very simple: occult nous and racy semen.

- 8 -

AS CANAVAN WENT about the country he was readied—in precisely the way that meat is readied when salted—by the saline taste of blood on his lips.

- 9 -

SERGEANT TOM BROWN steered the Primera in accordance with the stirrings of his chubby hands—call it feel, or divination. The almost half-century of his service had earned him an intuitive reading of an offender's rhythms. He recognised the moment when a long hiatus in activity might break with quick flurries, the way a run of successes might stiffen the blood and embolden, the way the odds that were chanced could suddenly steepen, and most of all he knew the feeling of an imminent violence: it caused a clamminess to his skin and upset in his tummy.

The feeling was on him now as he drove the sea road on this Sunday of mist and fear. His hatred of a Canavan—of this particular and of the type—permeated his senses. Everything was off—his vision so blurred the road signs were a squiggled Arabic; his hearing out of whack as though shot by thunderclaps—and everything would remain off until the bastard was caught and done for.

"He's not far," he said, and as he rode sucked honey from a squeezable tub.

- 10 -

A PENSIONER in an old farmhouse on the Mayo side of the mountain—picture it forlorn—had on the Thursday previous heard a midnight rustling: she lit the yard lamp to find the Canavan with a slash hook raised and a finger to his matinée lips.

He took four hundred euros and a phone charger and for badness's sake hit her a dig in the kidneys.

He had to be laid up someplace close.

- 11 -

THE WORRY for Sergeant Brown was that Canavan could lay up now the way a ferret will lay up in the burrow with the rabbit it has killed, the forked spit of its tongue lapping at neck blood, the pointed teeth taking tendon and bone apart, the claws carefully tearing back the skin—so tender the care, almost loving—to reveal the feast of vitals within, a feed that might last for days, and there is no way of getting the ferret out again short of extendable poles or dynamite.

- 12 -

BUT IT WAS merely patience that was required—a Canavan could not keep its snout down forever. It had to show itself always. The handsome dying face would seek again the light. Would take to dance floor or to bar stool. Would search out the windows left open against the humid spell or try the handles of the parked cars at the golf club. All a Sergeant Brown—the particular, the type—had to do was be patient and wait and gauge closely the stirrings in his hands.

- 13 -

FROM A BARMAN in Enniscrone he took first word of the widow—her new-build dormer, outside Easkey village, was the latest known Canavan hide.

When the sergeant got there, at teatime on the Sunday, she was alone and already bruised. She had the dead-eyed aura of drugs about her and there were raspberry-coloured thumb marks on her neck and shoulder.

"Ah, stupid," she said. "Stupid."

As he sat opposite her and peered closer he saw that the mouth, too, was lately busted. The bottom lip was beestung yet with a rude sexual swell. Tan makeup did not quite hide a bruising to the cheekbone.

"I'd it coming to me," she said.

Fucking eejit woman, the sergeant thought.

"How long were you knocking around with him, Sheila?"

Outside the sea rasped hoarsely; she rolled her eyes to show the whites.

"A while," she said, and there was the smell of whiskey off her, too, a bottle of High Commissioner nearing its last on the coffee table.

Blended scotch filth, the sergeant thought.

"Where's it he is now, Sheila?"

"I don't fucken know, do I?"

"I'd say different, Sheila."

"Can say what you fucken like."

"Has he left anything here?"

She acknowledged that he had and it was in a bedroom thick with an unmentionable musk that the sergeant went through Canavan's holdall—a Reebok with a busted zipper. It contained a phone charger, a pack of Nurofen painkillers, a change of sweatpants, and some briefs. The holdall was heartbreaking and the sadness it caused set the sergeant to his course.

He went back to her, as she poured the bottle's last,

and he eyed her carefully, and he was stirred for her and for the dying man both—their glow of life.

"Where's he?"

"I said I don't know."

The sergeant moved in beside her on the couch then, and slipped an arm around her shoulder, and clasped her tightly to him, and whispered why it was best that she tell.

"The treatment could help him yet, Sheila," he said.

She looked at him as a serpent might.

"Could be it's Keash Hill," she said. "The caves up there."

Breathing fatly, Tom Brown rose and made to leave the bright, impersonal dormer—its walls as thin as eggshells—where the widow had been fucked and beaten, and he knew, inarguably now, that within the shadow of the Ox a killing was imminent, and would occur before the country turned from dark into daylight again.

He considered the purplish thrill of her busted lip.

"That'd want a stitch," he said.

She threw hate at him as he left.

"Fuck off," she said.

\- 14 -

THE CAVES at Keash Hill were no more than a forty-minute haul from the Ox Mountains and there lay the remnants of elk, wolves, bear. It was a place haunted by desperate mammals since the hills and mountains had cracked and opened—as the province of Connacht formed—a place with a diabolic feeling sometimes along its shale and bracken stretches; a darkness that seeped not from above but from beneath.

Sergeant Brown parked on a side road and walked the ledged ascent—he held a palm to his heart for fear that it might at any moment give.

\- 15 -

THE HIGHER he climbed the more treacherous the ledges and just barely was the track a fat man's width. His small feet were nervous in tan brogues and swam greasily in their socks. The last of the long Sunday shed light for a half-darkness; the sky had deepened in the haze; the corduroy lines of its vapour trails wavered on the fade. The half-night was shadowland. A killing will name its time always and it had named it for now. He found the Canavan sitting outside the last and highest of the caves, sucking on a cigarette, blithely, with his legs hooked up beneath him, and aware fully that the killing time had been named, and that this time he could not wriggle free.

"Get up," the sergeant said.

The handsome eyes burned into the sergeant as he rose and Tom Brown wanted to belt him and he wanted to kiss him.

- 16 -

FOR THE SERGEANT there was no decision to be made. Take one of them and spare one of us—an act votive to his trade. As he led his captive down the ledges it took just the palm of a hand to the small of the back—a jolt and sudden force, and the Canavan was over the ledge, and falling, and the rocks below made quick silent work of the hazel eyes, the languor, the cancer.

- 17 -

THERE WAS NO VICTORY in it. Sergeant Brown knew as he drove the sea road home that each tiny light that burned on the Ox might burn to light a Canavan child, and it would be no time at all until he was in long pants, and no time at all until he was driving, and the sergeant would by then be cold and sober in the clay of Sligo, or at best in the coronary-care unit, and all that would be left to him would be the fear, which persists.

He feared now the summer night for its sly and sweet-found darkness, and he imagined on the night breeze a sardonic note, as though the Ox were taunting. These mountains, their insistences: those who would run would run and those who must follow must follow, and waiting—oh, wasn't there always—some heated girl, so wistful.

Listen?

The tinkled chime of her laugh against the mountain black as she feigns outrage at a dropped hand, and now—*listen*—the tiniest brushing of the air as her eyelashes close and bring down the darkness: the falling-in-love-all-over-again.

OLD STOCK

THE SPRING had been long and cold. The wind that came across the lake still had winter's bite and the house was wearing its age and ached loudly in the wind, as though poorly, and I was myself sick in the bowel, the gut, and the gums. Or the nerves, in other words. Or the soul. I badly needed to get out of County Sligo, and it was word of an imminent death that allowed me to.

EARLY IN MAY, the call came through that Uncle Aldo was on his way out up in Donegal. It was a miracle that he was even going still. Aldo had drank like a fool always and chased women and crashed cars; he burned summonses; he fell out of a hotel one time and landed on a taxi. I was the last of his close relations. He was my father's only brother, and my father was long dead. It was the lungs, in either case, that would cart them off. The lungs and the dampness, I suppose. Here's a very old joke—

Cause of Death: the west of Ireland.

ALDO HAD MOSTLY BEEN a figure of my childhood. His visits had been antic, unpredictable. I remember him one Christmas in plaster of Paris to the shoulder, lurching into the house, lame as an old pirate, a naggin of John Powers whiskey in his free paw; another time in the company of a foul-mouthed blind girl called Margaret; once so atrociously drunk he pissed in a corner of the guest bedroom and there was murder over it—my mother put him out of the house the next morning. But I had seen him infrequently in recent years and I was a little surprised that contact had been made at all and to be summoned to his deathbed like this.

I aimed the car north for Donegal and though my business was sombre, I felt a quiet soaring of the heart—I clearly welcomed this chance of a visit to the country outside Glenties, where my uncle was living out this last spell.

And yes it was very beautiful there. It was early in the Maytime, and there were dreamy glens and rooky woods, and all the rest of it, the mountains in their pure realm, and so forth, and being closer to the coast, the sky was clearer and the air that much quicker; the expanse of clean raw light was reviving.

And anyway Aldo was eighty-fucking-odd, I mean how devastated was I supposed to be?

HIS COTTAGE looked across a bog to the Bluestack Mountains; the ocean was nearby, unseen but palpable. There were huge granite boulders around the fields, as if giants had been tossing them about for sport. The ocean hissed at the edges of the scene like a busy gossip. There was salt on the air and the local cars wore coats of rust. I felt somehow a little hardier and tougher in myself as I looked out from the doorway of Aldo's place. I was in shade from the noon sunlight under the strands of a whitethorn's blossom. I rested its tiny flowers in the palm of my hand and blew on them.

"Bad luck, they say, to bring it into the house?"

The doctor smiled—

"Are you superstitious?"

"More so than I used to be, actually."

Once identified as family I had become in the usual way a functionary of the dying. I was consulted by the doctor and by a priest—Aldo had refused the hospital, abused the cleric. The doctor said there was only so much he could do. He murmured the usual words: we'll try to make him comfortable at least. Aldo was fixed to an oxygen rig-up. He was pumped full of the good stuff. He was in and out of consciousness.

"Hours rather than days," the doctor said.

And we agreed together in the native way that he'd nearly be as well off out of it.

HENCE TO THE DEATHBED—

Aldo was much reduced; he was a remnant of himself already. It was heartbreaking, actually. He was thrown back against a cast-iron bedstead, a nineteenth-century original that I reckoned at a glance you could sell for two, two and a half grand in Dublin. In fact, everything in the cottage was antique and beautifully functional and reeked of a kind of authenticity I had a great yearning for. Uncle Aldo told me at once—the oxygen mask ripped melodramatically from his face—that the place was to be mine.

"Ah Jesus, Aldo," I said. "That's too much."

He was going quickly. A new life yawned open before me. I looked out towards the Bluestacks, and I could hear the sea, and the mountains were hard-founded in the clear evening light.

WHEN HE COULD GET the words out, in these final hours, they came in quick lucid rushes—he was on his last visits back to himself—and he spoke mostly of old jobs, old adventures.

"I fucked a nun once in Moose Jaw," he said.

"Where's Moose Jaw?" I said.

"Canada," he said. "There was great money that time layin' tar in Canada. She was after hoppin' the convent wall of a Tuesday. This was the Thursday."

Once he woke and took me to be his brother but then as myself again. With a weak sweeping of the hand, he displayed the room around him, the house, my legacy.

"The place isn't worth tuppence," he said. "No point selling it."

He beckoned me to come closer—

"There could be a tumour the size of a small dog atein' you from the inside out," he said, "and you wouldn't even know it."

"Okay," I said.

"So what you should do," he said, "is live your fucken life."

"I have you now," I said.

"And I tell you," he said, "this place? Whatever way this house was set down . . . just here . . . on this spot . . . I can't explain it but the women go mental fucken gamey as soon they get a waft of the place at all."

With a surge of unnatural strength he clawed me towards his chest and rasped the words at me—

"Get them sat in there by a peat fire with a glass in their hand," he said, "and they can't keep the clothes on their backs."

AS HE DOZED OFF for a while—"dozed" may be a little pretty for what he was up to—I went outside and circled the cottage slowly. Aldo had a round of sally trees for a windbreak and they moved in the stiff breeze now to show charms of light. This place could wreak fucking havoc on a man's prose if you let it. Perhaps the austerity of south Sligo had been the saving of me—looking out at endless rain and reed fields, you are not inclined towards a curlicued or ornamental style. But here the aspect was glamorous and drunk-making. I went inside again, scared of it, and I examined the old crockery, the time-worn flags of the stone floor, the poignant maw of the original peasant fireplace. I went to find Aldo alert again but for the last time in his chamber.

"Your father was a strange drinker," he said. "Lazarus I used call him. He'd look to be on his way out after six or seven pints, kind of swayin' and half rollin' . . . But then suddenly he'd straighten the shoulders, suck down a bit of wind, and go again for another three or four hours . . . Looking at you like a judge."

"That was your father," he said.

ALDO—the complicated event now of his dying face. This tic, and that tiny wrenching, and what did this last cloud that passed across his straining eyes tell? Aldo, proud as a hawk and poor as a wren, the closing of the eyes, and then at once the final thing. And suddenly he was without life or pain.

I went outside. I had a rush of true feeling. This could be the place for me all right. Maybe the thin film of skin between me and the world would at last here be pierced. I would be at one with the natural things, with mountain, sky, and sea.

THERE IS A BELIEF, of course, that the love of nature is a type of spilt religion and to develop it later on in life, in one's forties, is suspicious stuff indeed. And there was something unseemly in the way that I was almost weeping with happiness as I walked the lyric fields and lanes in the blissful June evenings, but it was in this manner, over those slow weeks, that I mourned my uncle, and more than I would have expected to.

I FELL QUICKLY into a routine in my new home. I was neat as a sparrow about my days. I was up as it got bright. I no longer took the metaphorical whip to myself as soon as I woke. In fact, I treated myself like a lord. I had soda bread toasted and slathered heavily with butter, a pot of strong tea at its side. Sometimes I added a splash of cream to my porridge, sometimes a little whiskey. I listened without panic to the morning news. The world receded beautifully from my new hide in the northwest. It was a plain but luxuriant life in the well-swept cottage, with the door left open to a fine and thickening summer. A solicitor's office in Donegal town was on to me about the will and the deeds but I sailed through it all. Nothing was a bother to me here. I seemed to carry myself in a much calmer way. I was slow and deliberate about things. Suddenly I had an old farmer's patient style. I walked the narrow roads and waved stoically to passing strangers in holiday rentals. I was a reassuring presence, I felt, on these roads. On a peg on the back of the kitchen door I found an old cap of Aldo's—a proper Donegal tweed—and I perched it at a jaunty angle rising from my forehead. I began to get the sense that life is not much more than an inch or two deep, really—how you display the surface of things can dictate all else. I eased into my new skin. And I thought about Aldo plenty. The evenings could be a sad time—here I was among all his things. I believed that Aldo's talk of women had been no more than an old man's wishful thinking. He had been alone, lonely and sick here. The cottage was cold enough, even on these summer evenings, and I burned a few sticks for warmth and company. I drank not much, read sparingly—I had no great thirst, and I could not keep my eyes focused on the pages; I was encountering, I believed, some kind of transformation.

One night in January I had walked out of the Sligo house, crossed the reed fields, walked the greasy planks of the jetty and attempted to lower myself into the lake. It was the sheer iciness of the black water that forced me back. But then I suppose January is a tough month for everyone. Though maybe not to the extent that they try to fucking top themselves. Coming from a small family, I had not much support to summon by phone call, and I had consciously pulled away from my old friends. All of them. But now, in Donegal, in the clear light of summer,

I was somehow making amends with myself. I let the music play out late and low on Lyric FM. I had the sense that I was deflating the last of my old self, slow breath by slow breath.

THE SOLICITORS were on again. There were more forms to be signed. I said I'd drive down but this was not necessary—one of their team would be near Glenties on the Friday for the conveyancing of a farm and the forms could be dropped in to me.

It was a youngish solicitor who came by the cottage. She was attractive, quite dark, and with a Donegal accent like running velvet. She stood with me by the doorway, where the whitethorn gave shade and dangled its occult strands.

"And you'll not put it on the market?" she said.

"I might stay a while," I said.

She looked towards the kingdom ground of the Bluestacks across the way.

"There is something about this place," she said.

"Have you a long run back?" I said.

And yes, I told her, it was beautiful country, and the few people I'd met had seemed sweet-natured to me, and I was struck by the great produce available these days in the town markets nearby.

"Fantastic local cheeses," I said. "I could, ah . . . I could do you up a sandwich for the road?"

"Ah now," she said.

"I've a blue cheese from Ardara you'd weep for," I said.

"A blue?" she said.

"Dairy is my heroin," she said.

"I'll make it," I said. "Sure you can eat it here if you like."

I made for the kitchen before she could protest.

"And I must put a match to that fire," I said. "It gets cool enough still in the evenings."

When I served her the sandwich it was with an air of priestly decorum, and I said—

"You wouldn't take a drop of wine with that?"

A laugh rippled mischievously at the back of her slender throat.

"I suppose it is a Friday," she said.

We were in the bed inside an hour, and we horsed into each other then for the rest of the afternoon.

It was fabulous.

A SECOND MEETING was arranged. We had dinner in the town. A disaster. Our talk oozed out over the chowder with all the vitality of wet cement. As she gnawed at her steak, I saw that her teeth were a little crooked. There had already been a difficult moment when she ordered it well-done and I asked if she had a fear of blood, and it was possible that I had a haughty or even a sniggering tone. Away from Aldo's cottage, the level of my suavity was again in terrible deficit. There was no question of a third time out—the poor girl practically hurdled the waiter as she ran from the place. Maybe it had not been the best idea to get into my suicide attempt over the coffee.

I FOUND the ideal thing as the summer aged was to keep myself close to the cottage. But even then I wasn't safe from the intruding world. An Italian lady in hiker's gear called by one evening looking for directions and a refill of her water bottle. She nearly pushed the door in on top of me. I hadn't the tap running when she had her boots off by the fireplace and was massaging her toes, with her head lolling dangerously. There was no shifting her from the place. After a good hour, I stood up and outright asked her to leave and she rose up herself, flung me against the antique dresser and bit my chin. And sadly I succumbed to it all, again, on the floor, in front of the fireplace, and it went on (or maybe just seemed to) for fucking hours—shamefully, I had to fake a climax to put a stop to it.

Then before dawn she took me again.

THE WRITING was going tremendously. I was due to deliver my third novel. The central philosophy underpinning all of my work to date was that places exerted their own feelings—nonsense, of course, half-thought-out old guff that sounded okay at literary events but now, here in Aldo's cottage, there was incontrovertible evidence that it was the case. In this place I was calm, lucid, settled in my skin, and apparently ravishing. Elsewhere I was, as ever, a bag of spanners.

I packed up most of Aldo's old clothes for the charity shop in Glenties. I kept a tweed jacket, a few ties, the cap, some excellent brogues—we were a close enough match, size-wise: long, simian arms, short legs, no arses. I tried to breathe and settle. I bought little books that named the trees and the flowers of the vicinity. I drove out to Narin and Portnoo and swam in the cold seawater. My prose slowed down and took on a more sombre note; the third novel was apparently going to be all about family and landscape.

BUT AS THE SUMMER AGED, sleep became troublesome. I began to turn in the bed on the twist of strange groans I had never heard before. Had more been passed on from my uncle than I'd hoped for? Dark information rushed down the channels of the blood.

I found myself waking in deep unease and leaving the cottage in the middle of the night and walking the moonlit roads in the tweed jacket and cap and talking to myself in Aldo's scratchy voice and coarse tone. I was trying to outpace myself, in Aldo's stride, but sometimes, on those nights, I found that I was gaining again.

This was the other thing the work was going to be about—that there is no stepping away from the shadow of your past.

—

TO FACE MYSELF I would have to leave him go. I would have to move on again. I sold my car to a widowed lady from Portnoo. I had to physically restrain her from me when I was handing over the deeds under the whitethorn. I put the cottage on the market. I bought a small van and loaded it—I took the antique bedstead, the flagstones I had managed to pry loose, the fireplace surround, the crockery, anything that wasn't nailed down, and I aimed for Francis Street in Dublin and the antique places there.

There was no guilt at all. I knew well that I was a maggot, and that in my own unreliable ways I was precisely in the line of Aldo's stock, my reckless green-eyed uncle who had broken the hearts of nuns and blind girls, had stabbed friends in the shoulders if he missed their backs, had propositioned my mother in the scullery of an Easter Sunday morning, and who once had seen the lights of Moose Jaw burning across the Saskatchewan plain.

SAINT CATHERINE OF THE FIELDS

THE OLD SINGERS were all going. One by one they were vanishing from the map of the west. You could hear remnants of the music still but just faintly now from the lips of ancient women and men. I was trying to collect the songs that were as yet unrecorded before their moments had irretrievably passed. My research was in sean-nós—the "old style," in Irish—the unaccompanied folk singing that is plaintive, sometimes harsh, with often a lovelorn quality, and with narrative always. These were the song-stories that were usually passed down by means of the recital alone. One night in the summer, at a pub in the Inagh Valley in Connemara, I was told about a man called Jackson. He was a singer in south County Sligo and reputed to be a great collector. It was said that he had songs from deep in the nineteenth century even, songs that nobody else had now. My blood at once quickened but I could get nothing about this Jackson beyond his name and broad vicinity—the man who told me about him was really quite drunk.

Back home, however, an online search quickly offered a lead. In a university sean-nós vault, I found a song recorded in relatively recent times by a Jackson in County Sligo. It was titled "Amhrán Keash Corran" and sung by Timothy Jackson. The recording was from the late 1990s and he sounded old enough even by that stage. The song was nothing special in itself—a routine panegyric to place—but there was something in his voice that snagged me. He was a singer who would not relent. Google Maps reminded me that Keash Corran, or the Hill of Keash, rises in the Bricklieve Mountains, the rolling uplands that run west from Lough Arrow. I already knew the area somewhat from my endless criss-crossing of the provinces—it always had seemed to me quiet, haunted ground. A place of lakes that lay in greyness to answer their skies. A lonesome and promising territory, I thought.

—

ON A FREE WEEKEND in October, I drove out west from the city. The usual loosening occurred as I crossed the Shannon river. It's hard to describe it except as a feeling of openness that descends on me, a kind of receptivity. It's something I never experience in Dublin, as if certain signals are blocked to me there.

There wasn't a soul on the road in the village of Keash. In the early afternoon, its only pub, the Fox's Den, was shuttered, but a sign in the window advertised a session of traditional music for that same Saturday night. I checked into a B&B nearby. I tried to sleep for a while but my mind ran and I could not sleep. I went out to the foothills of the Bricklieves and walked the last of the day away. The hills displayed with arrogance the riches of autumn and glowed, and I walked in a state of almost blissful sadness. There had been an intense romance that lasted the first half of the year but it no longer held—she went back to her wife. At my age—I had long since cleared the vault of fifty—it was not unreasonable to assume that this might have been my last great love. But still my pain had that shimmer of bliss at its edges—I had gone to the end of passion with someone, once more, and I knew that the achievement was, as it always is, a quiet miracle.

THE MUSIC that night at the Fox's Den was finely played but familiar. I knew almost all of it. I drank but calmly enough. During a break in the session, I quietly cornered the box player at the bar, and I asked him did he know of an old fella called Timothy Jackson, a singer from the south county.

Ah God love us, he said. Sure poor Tim isn't great in himself at this stage.

I HAD NEARLY MISSED HIM. He was in a nursing home on the outskirts of Boyle, ten miles south from Keash. He was ninety-six and fading quick. I was his only visitor that bright October Sunday. Whoever was shaving the poor devil had their mind on other things. His skin hung roughly in folds like onion paper and his brittle jaw swung loose on the hinge. He no more than vacantly smiled in my direction but I talked away to him anyway. I told him of my interests and academic studies and of my great love for the music. Nothing came back from Jackson but the gurning of his dark, silent maw. Passing by on her rounds, the duty nurse was sympathetic, and she said to wait it out for a while—there were spurts of talk and life from the old man still. So I spoke to him some more. I said I was especially interested in songs native to his district and he seemed to become more animated at this, briefly, but he fell back again into the recesses of himself. By now the light was thickening in the window and I was about to give up on it and head back on the road to Dublin.

It was then that he started quietly to sing.

BACK IN THE CITY, in a fever of excitement, I broke off from the work that should have been occupying me and I brought the Tim Jackson recording onto the desk. Over the week that followed, I transcribed, with more than the usual difficulty, the twelve and a half minutes of the song that he had sung at the slow fading of Sunday afternoon, and that I had caught on my phone. It was delivered in an antique Connacht Irish and by its diction and phrasing I at once felt comfortable that it was pre-twentieth-century. It was hard to believe I had never come across the song before. It should have been a famously dark standard. It presented a very involved narrative and a most troubling story. All of human cruelty was contained within it but something, too, I thought, of what love means. In tone it was truly a one-off. The verses were charged with a kind of erotic mania that resonated all too sharply with my own contemporary funk. Its characters were deformed by desire, and thus the song blew familiar notes through the slutty arcades of my middle-aged brain. It was about lust, betrayal, sexual jealousy—it was meat and drink to me. It informed me that there had been others before as deranged by matters of the heart and loins as I was now.

This was a tremendous relief and consolation.

THERE WERE forty-two verses to the thing. I suppose the nights were long enough back then and wanted filling. I will try now to give the story of the song as plainly as I can.

The transcription in its first lines told that her name was Catherine Ryan, and that she was "álainn agus beag agus cothrom," and so she settled into my view as a small, attractive, blonde woman. She was born in low circumstances in the country of the Bricklieves. She knew its climbing paths as a fox knew them. She knew the sweet airs of the mountain fields. It was a great pain for her to leave the place. She left it when she was not much more than a girl. She went to the north of England and worked for years in a factory there. She married a man from the County Leitrim. He was a tallish rake and of merriment fond. They were both of them singers—"amhránaithe"—

and they sang the stars into the night above the slate roofs of Lancashire. They took to living by the night and became creatures of it. Their voices lifted and bounced from the tiles and brass of the heaving pubs. The nights turned them to a devilish kind of fun. A rogue pair, they fed off each other's mischief, and they were not long for the factory life. They were put out of their house. They were soon on the boat home to Ireland again.

AS THE SONG OPENED in this way, its verses felt so carefully textured and manipulated that I suspected a literary hand at work under the hood. The song achieved smooth temporal shifts but not blithely, for something of the story's passing scene was always given. The merest, glancing line gave somehow the sombre bricks and industrial smoke of England's Victorian north, and those brassy old pubs loomed above the verse, like lanterns in the dark of the long-lost singing nights. On the return to her home place, the eerie greys and solemn greens of mountain light came through, and the refraction of lake-light, too, a haze of mysterious expectation drawn from landscape and seeping into the story as she settled again into the world of the Bricklieves.

Quickly, on her return, she met the herdsman.

LANDLESS, without prospect of marriage or advance, he kept a suckler herd for a retired farmer up on the Bricklieves. Born to nearby Culfadda, he lived alone in the hills but for the cattle. He was a youngish man still and possessed of some innocence. He had never moved beyond the small circles of his world—the mountain, the cows, the occasional excitement of the mart and fair day. She met him on a fair day in the town of Ballymote. His natural shyness got past itself at the gaiety of her bright talk. She made him drunk with her talk. Her voice was musical, her eyes sharp and blue. She began from that day forth to climb the hill and call on the herdsman. She brought him fresh bread and news from below. The Leitrim rake was indifferent, it seemed, about his wife's visits to an unmarried man. After a short while—after the measure of a single moon, the verse tells us—the visits began to increase in frequency. Soon enough, the song suggests, she had the little boots worn out on herself she was up and down that hill so often. The prying eyes and minds of the locality were, of course, alerted to the visits. It was said that the duration of the visits increased—the locality quickly had a clock on the errant pair. The aching music of love was to be heard now across the hill, and the hill was not used to it. Leitrim was fully aware of the situation, a verse implies, and he was not at all put out by the cuckoldry. It became a great scandal and shame of the place but it was so scandalous, so beyond the realm of decency at that time, it was as if there was no language for it, and nothing was said—the vicinity of the Bricklieve mountains found itself in a condition of wordless outrage.

It felt as if the wind was holding its breath.

THE MATTER OF THE VERSES, at this point, switches to the effect of these events on the herdsman himself.

His world now was in a great tumult. This small, vivid, fair-haired presence in his life, and in his bachelor's bed, was utterly unexpected—it must have been like a visitation from another world. He woke up within himself and not pleasantly. He could feel the way the hot blood moved through him. He woke to the true and unexpected capacities of his heart, his awful capacities. He woke each day now to the previously unknown torments of love and desire. In fact, the song puts it more plainly, and in the true demotic language of the south county, and I can only honestly translate the sense of a particular line as follows—

The poor herdsman of Culfadda was cunt-struck.

SHE TOLD HIM that her husband was cruel to her but she could not leave him—if she left him, he would surely die. He came to believe in her almost religiously. When he said her name it was in an awed whisper and as if in litany. He came to see her as a saintly figure almost, his Saint Catherine, his saviour.

NOW THE COMPLICATIONS of the entanglement came to obsess the vicinity as they did the verses of the song. The people of the district tried to reason the story out. Leitrim was reckoned a handsome man but, in the way of good-looking men, it was supposed that he would quickly come to bore a woman. The herdsman was nothing to write home about in the looks department—plain and startled-looking, we're told—but he had a great sweetness of nature. Leitrim was "a bitter drop," the song suggested, while the man on the hill was "buttermilk." He was a man also who could listen to a woman. She called to him each day as their spring gave on to a loving summer. As their physical love grew more practised, its hours slowed and pleasures deepened. His herd was by the love affair orphaned and drifted gormlessly and all but wild across the hill. She could be heard to sing to him sometimes on those summer afternoons. (If there's any patch of happiness to be found walking on that hill now, I wonder if it might remain from the moments of her singing?) The herdsman grew accustomed to her caresses, and to her compliments, and he might even have come to believe, foolishly, that he deserved them.

Then, inside a year, without forewarning, she left him and destroyed him.

THE TURN in the song was drastic, quick, and ugly. The veils were ripped away from the verses. It was revealed to be a story of erotic wickedness and greed. The Leitrim husband had been in collusion all the while. It was no more than a sport for them. The herdsman was an object they used to bring an excitement darkly to their own coupling. She fed the husband every last morsel of those afternoons. The song tells us, in perhaps its most terrible verse, that he even came quietly up the hill sometimes to watch.

I could not but imagine the nights the plan of it was laid down, by lamps or by candlelight, the wicked spirit of the husband inhabiting and steering to foul design the willingness of his wife, the way they wrote the verses of it almost, the way the young herdsman who appeared on that fair day in Ballymote was drawn into being only by their shared and urgent carnal need. He could not have existed in the form that he took without them.

Love, we are reminded, yet again, is not about staring into each other's eyes; love is about staring out together in the same direction, even if the gaze has menace or badness underlain.

Do you mean that I am going to be left? the herdsman said.

THE TRANSCRIPTION was not yet complete but already I was in a terrible state. I got up from the desk and rolled the blind and looked out to the north Dublin night. Hours had passed by since I sat down to work on the closing verses. The lights of the estates burned coldly in the silence of midnight; beyond were the lights of the airport fields. I thought about ringing Karen and trying to explain what had gone wrong with us earlier in the year. But the prospect of standing there, at fifty-four years of age, with the phone in my hand, husky of voice, passion's slave—it was too much. Anyway, as the song made clear, we have no agency in our romantic manoeuvres—the decisions are all made for us, without our even knowing. The decisions are out there already, on the air.

And beneath the lights of the city all those people were out there, being born and dying, and steered in their unknowing, all the way from the first moment to the last.

THE WOMAN from the Bricklieves came to me that same night in a dream. I saw her advancing out of the darkness—she was lithe, blonde, and agile. She had a terrible utterance on her lips as she came towards me, and a kind of madness in her eyes. It was as if she meant to do me harm, and I retreated backwards into my sleep, step by careful step.

Maybe she was just aware that her own time was so pinched and mean. Maybe all she wanted was as much of what that mean life could give.

IN THE BRICKLIEVE HILLS, so long ago now, the herdsman wanted nothing more than for his life to end but it would not end. He had so many years left to imagine her. Her movement, her taste, and the slur of indecipherable words that emerged when she lay in a half-sleep after lovemaking. There were decades yet in which his destruction would continue, day by day, night by night, cell by cell. She never darkened the climbing path to call on him again. He never saw her face coloured by the sunlight of those mountain fields again. If he had, he would have at once forgiven her—this was the sentence passed down for the sin of his adoration.

It is the herdsman that takes us out of this sorrowful piece but as my head fell onto the desk, all wrung-out and wretched, the song's closing plea might as well have been issued as my own—

Oh lie with me once more, my love, if only for the last time.

TORONTO AND THE STATE OF GRACE

THE WINTER BLEEDS us out here. These December mornings, it is often just myself and the dead jellyfish who are left to the beach. These are the lion's mane corpses that get washed in on the equinoctial gales and they come in terrible numbers some years, as if there's been a genocide out there. They look like pink foetal messes flung about the sand and rocks—kids call the place the abortion beach—and the corpses are so preserved in the winter air they're a long time rotting down. How the soul lifts on the morning stroll. Then there's the endless afternoon to contend with—mostly, I have the bar to just myself and the radio, and we sit there and drone at each other. Maybe there's a lone customer, a depressed old farmer down from the hills, or maybe, the odd day, there are two. I am at this stage largely beyond caring.

But it was on just such a lifeless and dreary winter day, almost precisely as our ten streetlamps came on to glow against the dusk, that the rental car pulled up outside. I could hear two voices raised in an odd, quivery singing, but the voices ceased as the engine cut. A slight man in late middle age stepped out and braced himself against the evening chill. He looked at the sign above my door—it reads *Sullivan,* still, though it's years since there's been a Sullivan here. He came around the car and opened the passenger door and a frail bird-faced old dear in furs emerged. He offered an arm but she was proud to manage without. They stepped up together to stare through my window and their eyes were lit so madly that my breath caught in forewarning.

They entered my pub like a squall of hectic weather. There was a kind of cheerful eeriness about them. They took grinning to the bar stools. He swivelled a half-turn and squinted as he read the spirit labels—

"It's an attractive selection, Mother," he said.

"Let's not be rash, Tony," she said.

But she swivelled a half-turn, too, and hers drew a slow creak to the room that sounded in a crescent-moon shape, ominously.

"We'll work our way across the toppermost states," he said.

"Oh, Tony," she said. "Riding the Empire Builder? Again?"

He half rose from his stool, crooned a verse from "The Black Hills of Dakota," fell back again. He was fey and thin and whippety; she had the remnants of a sharp-boned beauty yet.

"He's a dreadful child but kind," she confided, and she laid her touch to the back of my hand where it gripped with white knuckles the bar top. Hers was paper-brown and cut deep with wrinkles.

"A Laphroaig to set us off from the station," he said, sitting again. "Let's strap ourselves in, dear."

"Laphroaig, Tony? Is that the peaty number?"

"Like drinking the bloody fireplace," he said.

"Two?"

"Water to the side," he said.

I set them and they sipped, and they considered each other with the same liquid eyes, and relaxed.

"Have you travelled far today?"

"Oh Christ," he said. "Was it Kenmare, Mother? Was the last place?"

"Horrendous," she said, and placed thin fingers to her throat in long suffering.

"Full of horrible skinny Italians on bicycles," he said. "Calves on like knitting needles and their rude bits in Lycra. I mean it's bloody December!"

"In fact," she said, "we were rather run out of town."

"There was an incident," he confirmed, "over supper."

"Last night?" she said. "We're barely in the door and there's talk of the guards."

"Five-star melodrama," he said. "Matinée and evening performances."

"We had . . . stopped off," she said. "En route."

"We were a little . . . tired," he said.

"We thought we'd take things more gently today," she said.

"Nonsense," he said. "We're riding the Empire Builder. We're taking the high ground. Is that a Cork gin I see?"

It was second along the line of optics from the Laphroaig—I thought, surely they can't be in earnest? There was a line of nine spirits turned and hung along there.

"Mine's with just the tiniest drizzle of soda water," she said.

"Mine's a slice of lime, if you have it," he said.

"To be honest . . ."

"Surprise me," he said. "Straight up is fine. Though I may become poisonous and embittered."

"Given you've a head start," she said.

"Do you see now?" he said. "Do you see now what I'm dealing with?"

I tried for what I imagined was a half-smile and set their gins.

"One yourself?" he said.

"I don't, actually."

Sobriety was the mean violet of dusk through the bar's window; the mean view down the falling fields to the never-ending sea; the violet of another mean winter for me.

"Toronto!" she cried.

"Oh Mother," he said. "It's barely gone five."

"Anthony was conceived in Toronto," she said. "I was Ophelia to Daddy's Prince. We're talking 1953, barman."

He didn't look sixty. He had the faded yellowish skin tone of a preserved lemon. Pickled, I suppose is what I'm trying to say, but it seems unkind.

THEIR MOODS came and went with each sip as it was taken. He took a sullen turn on the Cork gin—

"Kenmare was the fucking horrors," he said. "I had one of my spells."

"He hasn't had a spell since September," she said. "Not saying October was a picnic."

"Five this morning?" he said. "I'm lying in the bed, my heart is going like gangbusters, and there are bloody crows on the roof—crows! And they're at their screeching and their bloody cawing and the worst of it is I can make out the words."

I couldn't but ask—

"You don't want to know," he said. "Suffice to say I've always suspected the worst of crows."

"A crow is a crow," she flapped a wrist. "It's the rooks you want to watch out for."

"Oh, a rook knows," he said.

"Knows?"

"The day and the hour," he said.

"Sleep is a thing of the past for me," she said. "You'll find this as you get older, boys."

The bar was empty but for them. I just wanted to lock up for the day and not open for the night. I wanted to drink mint tea upstairs and watch television and go on the internet. But they were making light work of the Cork gin.

"It was a dry town," she said, narrowing her eyes, "was Toronto."

"Hideous Protestant bastards," he said. "What's this is next along?"

I turned, coldly; I tried to look stern.

"I'm afraid that's a very cheap and nasty Spanish brandy."

"How did you know I was coming?" he said.

THE MOVING SEA GLEAMED; it moved its lights in a black glister; it moved rustily on its cables.

"Of course Daddy was several years senior to me," she said. "I was a young Ophelia. He was an old Prince. Oh but *impressive.* He had range, had Daddy."

"Do you realise," he said, "that my father was born in 1889?"

"My goodness."

"Picture it," he said, swirling the last of his gin and signalling for two brandies; she'd already finished hers and had her palms placed expectantly on the bar top.

"1889," he said. "This was in County Mayo. In a cabin, no less, and in low circumstances. A whore mother bleeding down the thighs and seventeen screaming bastards swinging from the rafters . . ."

"Anthony," she said. "Really."

"To even emerge from such a milieu," he said, "walking upright and not on all fours speaks of something heroic in the old lech."

"He carried himself well," she said. "Daddy had class always."

"Meaning?" he said.

"Apples and trees, dear," she said. "You've got some, too."

"Some?" he said.

Together they tested their brandies with tentative lips.

"Coca-Cola," she said, and I set a small bottle for a mixer.

"I shouldn't," he said. "The caffeine doesn't agree with me."

He took a hard nip from his Spanish—suspiciously—but smiled then and looked up with new glee and blew the room a kiss. He slithered from the bar stool, began to hum an old romantic tune that was somehow familiar to me, and waltzed a slow-shoed shuffle as though with his own ghost.

"Julio Iglesias," she said.

The door opened and one of my poor farmers poked a glance in—Tony sang to him and pointed as he waltzed towards the door—my farmer turned and moved off down the village, sharpish.

Tony grabbed the door and shouted to the night after him—

"Come back at half past eight, darling! I'll be doing my Burl Ives!"

The chill of the evening faded again as he let the door swing closed and he took happily to his bar stool.

"Toronto?" she said. "The house was half empty most nights but the company was lively."

"Evidently," he said.

"I think it happened the very first time," she said. "He'd got his hands on a bathtub gin, had Daddy."

"The telling detail," he said.

"Tasted like turps," she said, "but it did make one pleasantly lightheaded."

He squinted again at the line of optics and shook his head.

"Now my wife?" he said.

"Don't, Tony," she said.

"Oh and by the way," he said. "What did you say your name was?"

"I didn't. I'm Alan."

"Well, Al," he said, "it turns out that my darling wife has only taken off with the Pilates instructor. A she. And twice the man I'll ever be."

"You should never have married an actress, darling."

"So you've been saying this last fourteen years, Mother."

"Marry the shop girl," she said. "Marry the factory line. Marry the barmaid. MARRY THE WHORE! But never, never marry the actress, Tony."

"Well, it's a little late for it, Mother."

"Of course in Toronto," she said, "there wasn't a great deal to do in the evenings. And the show'd finish for seven!"

"He gave her one down the fish dock."

"Oh Tony," she said.

"By the mighty Ontario," he said.

"Folks," I said, "listen, I mean really . . ."

"County Mayo–style," he said. "You know what I mean, soldier?"

"Tony," she said, disappointedly.

"As for my betrothed? I said, Well! I said, This Pilates has given you a whole new lease of life, Martina. You've come in glowing and you're up to four sessions a week."

"What's this is next along the line, Andy?"

"Alan," I said, and submitted to my fate. The way they moved was sure as a tide.

"It's an Absolut vodka," I said.

"Marvellous," he said. "One minute we're rock-chewing Spanish peasants humping the donkey in a humid night wind . . ."

"Humid!" she cried.

". . . the next we're on the porch of the dacha, it's a summer's evening, placid . . ."

"Placid," she said. "A light breeze licking the trees."

"Pine-scented secrets," he said. "Cruel handsome souls with cheekbones like knives. Burly intrigue . . ."

"Burl Ives," she said.

". . . and some rather fetching Cossack-type headgear. A tubercular old sort about to hack his last . . ."

I poured and set the vodkas over ice—they slammed them back neat.

"Of course Martina's not been right since the change," he said.

"Her manners are learned," said his mother. "There was always something forced about her manners. As if she'd learned them by heart. From a library book."

"Pilates!" he cried. "If it wasn't for the kiddies, it'd be a clean break."

"The kiddies were a disaster," she said. "At your age? I don't know what you were thinking, Anthony."

"Prolonging the noble line," he said. "1889 . . . Oh . . . Is that a Drambuie, Adam?"

THE ALCOHOL appeared really to have no great effect—it just kept them moving at a spinning clip.

"He never talked about Mayo much, Daddy," she said.

"You could hardly blame the man," he said.

"Though he told a horrid tale. About the day his father decided that *his* wife, Daddy's mother, was a brasser type, essentially. He stood at the bottom of the stairs and screamed the foullest abuse up at her. Then she flung a loaf of bread down and hit him on the head. Your daddy, as a kiddie, is watching the whole thing from under a table. The poor infant! And next *his* daddy flings the bread back up again and roars . . ."

She half stood on the bar stool and reddened as she called the line—

"'Feed your fucking bastards with it!'"

"Is it any wonder I turned out the way I did?" Tony said.

"Folks," I said. "In truth, I'm not feeling the best this evening, I think it's a virusy thing and I may lock up a little earlier . . ."

"Mine's a Drambuie, Al," she said.

"Times two," he said.

I set the glasses and poured.

"He talked about that loaf of bread for sixty years," she said.

"Martina and I? That first weekend? We never left the bed. Of course this was the eighties and we were extremely tanned and fit. Tenerife, matinées and evenings? That'll keep you in your skinny jeans."

"Always it would come up," she said. "The morning it all went bananas. Back in Mayo. Back in the . . . Was it a cottage, Tony?"

"It was a cabin."

"From what I could gather that was the last he ever saw of his father. The morning of the loaf of bread flung."

IT WAS BY NOW fully night outside; the road was deserted.

"Daddy did a turn," she said. "In his day. As a lady?"

"Oh?"

"Coeur d'Alene," she said. "We were hired for the Empire Builder. Lounge-car floorshow. 1957. Oh and Daddy was at his peak! This was before the tragedy, of course. He went as Dame Delilah. He was got up buxom. He was got up blonde. Tony was still on the bottle. Tony was still in the cot but it seeps in, does talent."

"I was four," he said, and a tiny tear came. "Riding the High Line!"

"I'll admit Daddy's nerves were not right," she said.

"What he'd been through, the trauma? He had . . . He had what I used to call his *things*. Which were something like Anthony's spells, actually. Come to think of it. But Daddy? Well! For example, he couldn't see a shoe on a bed. If he saw a shoe on a bed, he wouldn't be right for weeks."

"A shoe on a bed? This is new to me," he said.

"You were four," she said.

"Now I'm going to have a thing," he said, "about shoes on beds."

She smiled, and she rose up suddenly, at the shoulders, and her eyes brightened ever more gladly, and she gasped her last. Then she keeled over dead onto my bar counter. There was no question about it. The way her head snapped onto the countertop. She just went. There was no question of a passing out; there was no question of the one too many. This was Death on the premises. A single hard snap of bone on wood. He looked at her. He looked at me. He looked at her again, and coldly—

"Oh you haven't," he said.

THE ONE ROAD along the peninsula is a bad one, and we are at least a half-hour from Castletown of a winter's night. Which is an ignoble length of time for a woman dead on a bar stool. Together we carried her to the lounge seating and laid her out crookedly there. Her knees wouldn't straighten. I went upstairs to get a sheet. I didn't know what I was thinking or doing. I was panicked. I fetched a brown paper bag to breathe in. I took the sheet off the bed; it was like wrestling an octopus. But it covered her, at least, and I spoke stupidly then, intemperately—

"I suppose the shock would tend to sober you."

"Oh no," Tony said. "I'm still roaringly drunk."

He looked up at the optics.

"Where were we, Al?"

Next along the line was a Baileys, and I poured a pair of them over ice, and I sat with him on the lounge chairs as we sipped.

"They must have been happy in Toronto," he said. "Or at least had some kind of fuck glow."

From the gap in the mountain the ambulance was seen at last to spin its lights and to call out and as quickly again its men were in the door and about us. Tony went in the back of the ambulance with his mother. The last that I saw, his head was bobbing in the moving light as he yapped and cried and gesticulated.

I went upstairs with the rest of the bottle of Baileys poured into a pint glass filled with ice. I googled toxicology reports and I googled liability. I googled the Empire Builder and I could hear it as it moved across the mountains and the plains—

Winona.

Wolf Point.

Coeur d'Alene.

I had to get out for a bit. I walked down the cold road to the beach and it was just me and the dead jellyfish and my eyes stung with cold and all the silvers of the sea came and entered me there on the white sand like the surface of the moon pocked and cratered and the jellyfish lay dead and translucent all around me and I just lay where I had fallen into this night of void and stars and I thought oh Jesus, oh God, it's so fucking cold now.

WHO'S-DEAD McCARTHY

YOU'D SEE HIM COMING on O'Connell Street—the hanging jaws, the woeful trudge, the load. You'd cross the road to avoid him but he'd have spotted you, and he would draw you into him. The wind would travel up Bedford Row from the Shannon to take the skin off us and add emphasis to the misery. The main drag was the daily parade for his morbidity. Limerick, in the bone evil of its winter, and here came Con McCarthy, haunted-looking, in his enormous, suffering overcoat. The way he sidled in, with the long, pale face, and the hot, emotional eyes.

"Did you hear who's dead?" he whispered.

Con McCarthy was our connoisseur of death. He was its most knowing expert, its deftest elaborater. There was no death too insignificant for his delectation. A ninety-six-year-old poor dear in Thomondgate with the lungs papery as moths' wings and the maplines of the years cracking her lips as she whispered her feeble last in the night—Con would have word of it by the breakfast, and he would be up and down the street, his sad recital perfecting as he went.

"Elsie Sheedy?" he'd try. "You must have known poor Elsie. With the skaw leg and the little sparrow's chin? I suppose she hadn't been out much this last while. She was a good age now but I mean Jesus, all the same, Elsie? Gone?"

His eyes might turn slowly upwards here, as though in trail of the ascending Elsie.

"She'd have been at the Stella Bingo often," he'd reminisce, with the whites of the eyes showing. "Tuesdays and Thursdays. Until the leg gave out altogether and the balance went. She used to get whiteouts coming over the bridge. At one time she took the money for the tickets below at the roller disco. Inside in the little cage. Of course that wasn't today nor yesterday."

"Ah no, Con. No. I didn't know her."

In truth, he might have no more than clapped eyes on the woman the odd time himself, but still he would retreat back into the folds of the overcoat, like a flowerhead closing when the sun goes in, and he was genuinely moved by the old lady's passing.

Con McCarthy's city was disappearing all around him.

HE HAD A SPECIAL RELISH, it seemed to me, for the slapstick death. He'd come sauntering along at noon of day, now almost jaunty with the sadness, the eyes wet and wide, and he'd lean into you, and he might even have to place a palm to your shoulder to steady himself against the terrible excitement of it all.

"Can you believe it?" he said. "A stepladder?"

"Which was this, Con?"

"Did you not hear?"

"No, Con."

"Did you not hear who's dead?"

"Who, Con? Who?"

"Charlie Small."

"Ah, stop."

"The way it happened," he said, shaking his head against what was almost a grin. "They hadn't painted the front room since 1987. Now it isn't me that's saying this, it's the man's wife is saying this, it's Betty is saying this. She could remember it was 1987 on account of her uncle, Paddy, was home for his fiftieth. He was a fitter in Earl's Court. Since dead himself. Drowned in his own fluids, apparently. Betty was a Mullane from Weston originally. They were never toppers in the lung department. Anyhow. Charlie Small says listen, it's gone beyond the thirty-year mark, we'll paint that flippin' front room. Of course Betty's delighted. We'll get a man in, she says. No, Charlie says, it's only a small room, I'll have it done before the dinner if I start after the nine in the mornin' news. Betty strides out for a tin of paint. She comes back with a class of a peach tone. Lovely. Calming, that'll be, she thinks, not knowing, God love her, what's coming next, the stepladder being dragged out from under the stairs, Charlie climbing up to the top step of it, and the man ate alive from the inside out by type-2 diabetes and weakish, I suppose, on account of it and the next thing the dog's let in when it shouldn't be let in, and that little dog is saucy now, she always has been, and she goes harin' through the front room, a spaniel breed, unpredictable, and the tin of peach-coloured paint is sent flying and Charlie reaches out for it but the ladder's not set right and wobbles and next thing he's over and off the back of it and the neck is broke on the man."

He shook his head with a blend that spoke curiously of tragic fate and happy awe.

"Dead on the floor before they got to him," he said.

"Jesus Christ, Con."

"The day nor the hour," he said, and he walked away happily into the persistent rain.

HE HAD ABOUT forty different faces. He would arrange his face to match precisely the tang or timbre of the death described. For the death of a child Con McCarthy's woe was fathoms deep and painfully genuine. An early death in adulthood brought a species of pinched grief about his temples, a migraine's whine its music. He avoided eye contact if it was a drowning that had occurred—he had an altogether dim view of the Shannon river as an utter death magnet, and he was all too often to be found down in Poor Man's Kilkee, looking out over the water, wordlessly but his lips moving, as if in silent consultation with the souls that hovered above the river, their roar at the Curragower Falls.

HIS ROLE as our messenger of death along the length of O'Connell Street and back seemed to be of a tradition. Such a figure has perhaps always walked the long plain mile of the street and spoken the necessary words, a grim but vital player in the life of a small city. But Con McCarthy's interest in death was wide-ranging, and it vaulted the city walls, so to speak, and stretched out to the world beyond to gorge intimately upon the deaths of strangers.

"Here's one for you," he said, leaning into me one day outside the George Hotel. "Man in Argentina, I believe it was. Cattle farmer. Impaled on his own bull. And didn't the bull go mental after it and charged in circles around the field ninety mile an hour and the poor farmer still attached to the horns with the life bled out of him. An hour and a half before a neighbour was got over with a shotgun, that long before they shot the bull and got the misfortunate corpse off the horns. Can you imagine it? The man's wife and children were watching, apparently. Roaring out of them. They'll never be right."

Another day, creeping up behind me, with a light touch to my elbow, and then the lean-in, the soft whisper, and here was news of the famous dead . . .

"Zsa Zsa Gabor," he said. "Gone. Though I suppose it was nearly a release to the poor woman for a finish. Did you know she'd been five year on life support?"

"That I did not know, Con."

"Five year. Heart attack at the end of it. Sure the poor

heart would be weak as a little bird's in the woman's chest at that stage. I believe it was ninety-nine years of age she was. They're after plantin' her in a gold box outside in California. No woman deserve it more. A former Miss Hungary."

HAD HE BEEN EXPOSED to death early? I wondered. Was it that some psychic wound had been opened at first glance into the void? Whatever the case, I believed that his condition was worsening. He began to move out from actual occurrences of death to consider in advance the shapes it might yet assume. Walking down the street now he was reading death into situations. He was seeing it everywhere. He had the realisation we all have but that most of us are wise enough to keep submerged—the knowledge that death always is close by. He'd stop to consider a building site. He'd look up. The long, creased face would fold into a hopeless smile, and as you passed by, he'd lean in, the head slowly shaking.

"Are you not watching?" he said.

"Which, Con?"

"See that scaffold above there? Are you not watching the wind on it? If that wind gets up at all, the whole lot could come down. A pole could go swingin'. Open your head and you walking down the road as quick as it'd look at you. And that would be an end to it."

HE WALKED THE CIRCUIT of the three bridges every night. If you idled anywhere by the river of an evening you might take the slow rake of Con McCarthy's worried eye. He would try to have a good read of you. I met him one night on the far side of the river. He was on a bench, the water moving slowly past, the traffic scant but passing its few lights across the falling dark. Maybe it was the September of the year. That sense of turn and grim resolve about the days, the evenings.

"Did you not hear?" he said.

"Ah, which was this, Con?"

"Did you not hear who's dead?"

"Who, Con? Who?"

But this time he just grinned, as if he was playing with me, and he let the weak-tea smile play out loosely across the river a few moments.

"Ah sure look," he said. "We're all on the way out."

"I know, Con. I know."

"Isn't that the truth of it? For a finish?"

"Can I talk to you seriously, Con?"

"Hah?"

"Can I ask you something?"

"What?"

"Why are you so drawn to it? To death? Why are you always the first with the bad news? Do you not realise, Con, that people cross the road when they see you coming? You put the hearts sideways in us. Oh Jesus Christ, here he comes, we think, here comes Who's-Dead McCarthy. Who has he put in the ground for us today?"

"I can't help it," he said. "I find it very . . . impressive."

"Impressive?"

"That there's no gainsaying it. That no one has the answer to it. That we all have to face into the room with it at the end of the day and there's not one of us can make the report after."

I BECAME MORBIDLY fascinated by Con McCarthy. I asked around the town about him. I came to understand that he was in many ways a mysterious figure. Some said he came from Hyde Road, others from Ballynanty. The city was just about big enough to afford a measure of anonymity. You could be a great familiar of O'Connell Street but relatively unknown beyond the normal hours of the day and night. We might know broadly of your standing, your people and their afflictions, but the view would be fuzzy, the detail blurred. So it was with Con. He did not seem to hold down a job. (It was hard to imagine the workmates who could suffer him.) His occupation, plainly, was with the dead. It was difficult to age him. He was a man out of time somehow. The overcoat was vast and worn at all seasons and made him a figure from a Jack B. Yeats painting or an old Russian novel. There was something antique in his bearing. The rain that he drew down upon himself seemed to be an old, old rain. One night on William Street, I spotted him sitting late and alone in the Burgerland there over a paper cup of tea.

That cup of tea was the saddest thing I ever saw. I sat in a few tables from him and watched carefully. As he sat alone his lips again moved and I have no doubt that it was a litany of names he was reciting, the names of the dead, but just barely, just a whisper enough to hoist those names that they might float above the lamps of the city.

AND MAYBE he was truly the sanest of us, I sometimes thought, on those nights in October when I could not sleep, and I took to driving late around the streets and the bridges and the town, and I knew that it was passing from me, and how remarkable it was that we can turn our minds from that which is inevitable—Con McCarthy could not turn from it. As cars came towards me at pace on the dual carriageway, sometimes for just the splinter of a moment there in the small hours I wanted to swerve and jolt into their lights and bring the taste of it onto me, the taste of its metal on my lips. Bring forward the news even if I could make no subsequent report of it.

When Con McCarthy died it was, of course, to a

spectacular absence of fanfare—suddenly, unexpectedly, and rating no more than a brief line in the Chronicle "Deaths" of a Tuesday in November.

Almost laughing, almost glad, I went along O'Connell Street in the rain with it; I leant in, I whispered; and softly like funeral doves I let my suffering eyes ascend . . .

"Did you hear at all?" I said. "Did you not hear who's dead?"

ROMA KID

SHE WATCHED her brothers sleeping but not for long and left them in the grey dimness of a February morning that was not yet half to life. She did not speak the language but understood plainly the knotted gestures and the dull faces of the people that worked here. Her mother had told her nothing but the girl knew that soon the fam ily would be sent home again and she would not go back there. She was nine years old and chose for her leaving the red pattern dress and zipped her anorak over it.

She went quietly among the chalets of the asylum park. She held the zipper of the anorak between her lips and its cold metal stuck fast to her lips. It was a ritual of safe passage to hold it there until she was clear of the park. She did not look back at all and no voices rose to call her back. She walked out to the foreignness of the morning. She climbed the embankment. She had none of the words that appeared on the advertising boards by the motorway as she walked in her squeaking trainers along its verges. She did not have the words on the side of the bus that passed by lit against the morning and she had none of the pitying words that formed on the mouths of the passengers who stared out at the thin child in a dress of red paisley, an anorak—

Poor knacker child.

Poor pavee kid.

Poor latchiko.

She walked for an hour or more. She was hungry. She knew where to cross for the station by the image of a train on the road sign and by the arrow's direction. There were people at the station waiting in a yellow heated room. She did not ask them for money because if she did not speak there was a good chance she would not be spoken to. Her stomach hissed and the morning sent up its first cuts of lonesomeness and fear. She would not see her brothers again.

Slight as a ghost she went about the station as its haunting. She knew by the one journey the family had taken that the trains aiming left must be headed back to the city of Dublin again, and to its trouble, and those that aimed contrary must go to the countryside beyond. There was no ticket checker at the station—it was a man on the train that checked the tickets and on the outward journey he had been a kind man and on the fact of this kindness she had built her plan and laid her fate.

She crossed the rails by the metal bridge. A light rain began to fall and it spoke more than anything else of the place through which she moved. There were just a couple of passengers waiting on the far platform. Her trust also was that the countryside would be kinder.

As she sat on a bench she felt again for the zipper of her anorak and got it between her teeth and bit down hard on it. When she had played with her brothers the evening before, it was for the last time, and they had fallen one by one to sleep then, and she counted off in her mind once again, and as she would for many years, the four black buttons of their tiny bopping heads: Andrzej, Luca, Tobar, Bo, the way there was a tune to it almost.

The minutes passed and the platform became busier. Tired-looking men and women took their morning places on the platform and let down slow ropes of words. She listened intently for the tone that might signal danger but the people were too tired to notice her, or at least they did not notice her for long: she registered for half a second's pity or distrust—poor Roma kid—and was erased again.

The train's noise came up as a rumble of promise. The word on the bulb of the train's nose was *Sligo*. The morning came alive around her as the train pulled in and she watched herself as though from above as she climbed on board. She stayed in the space between two carriages. The train took off again and she rocked on her heels as she crouched there. There were many empty seats but she did not enter a carriage to take one. As she crouched and rocked she began to sound a low groaning beneath her breath, and she let it sustain, and it slowed the beating of her heart, and it made her feel stronger. She blinked her eyes also, rapidly, and in a rhythm counter to the low, held groaning—she made in this way a shield of hummed noise and flickered movement against the world and its grey morning.

The train pulled back the morning and the countryside and she was alert to the grey fields passing, to the sheds and outbuildings, the sidings and high, the distant towns, and as she went by she checked for possible hiding places and lairs. She was reassured. She was very hungry.

Drawn by her hunger a cart came trundling along the passage laden with sandwiches and cakes and crisps and cans of soft drinks. The cart was pushed by a young woman and the girl knew at a glance she was not from this country either. The woman searched her out quickly with a look, and said—

Okay?

The girl was frightened at the day's first contact but smiled and something in the smile was read by the woman.

Are you alone? she said. You speak English?

She knew the word "English" and shook her head against it.

The woman spoke in another language then and it was closer but not known and again the girl shook her head and with her large eyes she pleaded.

Don't be frightened, the woman said.

She passed the girl a muffin and moved on again and as the girl held in her hand the muffin she held her breath also.

She waited, and then she took off the plastic wrapper, and the doughy smell came up like heat and there was the smeared blue of the berries, and she broke off precisely a quarter piece, and wrapped the rest again carefully, and placed it in the pocket of her anorak. Even as she savoured the first bite she was already patting her pocket to be sure the rest of the muffin was in place. The creatures in her stomach were soothed and quietened as she chewed.

She kept watch along the carriages for the ticket collector. After a couple of stops the train was almost empty. The wind moved in slow waves across the winter fields;

there was the iron beat of movement along the line. She was lulled, and she closed her eyes for a half-minute, and then more—she tried not to go deep—but she drifted, and almost dreaming she felt the soft pads of fingertips on the back of her hand. She opened her eyes to the ticket collector—

Now, he said.

By the word she could not yet tell if he was kind or not. She shook her head, and pleaded.

Uh-oh, he said.

She knew what that meant.

Are you not with somebody? he said.

No mother? he said. No father?

She bit down hard on her bottom lip.

Okay, he said.

The nine years of her life were written on the fibres of her skin and she could be plainly read. All the alleys and doorways and pleading years could be read, and the longing for the four tiny brothers who had been her comfort and, guiltily, her burden—their black buttons of heads, bopping—and the cold tile floors of railway stations, the detention chalets, the home place that would not be seen again, the cherry brandy on her grandmother's sour breath, the softness of her father's touch; all could be read.

Do you know where you are even?

Silently, she pleaded.

We're past Longford now, he said. Have you people waiting on you? I'm not even going to ask about a ticket.

He made the gesture of scratching his head and she smiled as he played at being puzzled.

What'll we do with you at all? Hah?

The food cart at that moment came by again. She was the subject now of a consultation. The ticket man conferred with the woman who pushed the cart. After a moment, both of their heads moved sadly from side to side. A phone call was made.

The train pulled into a country station. The doors gasped and opened, and the treetops outside were eerie with the voices of birds. She hummed a low groaning and flicked rapidly her eyelids.

Go handy now, the ticket man said.

She was made to leave the train. She was placed in the station master's care. He brought her to a room of the station house that was made up as a home.

What in Jesus' name are we going to do with you? he said, as the colour rose and then faded in his face again.

He gave her a banana and some biscuits. He went to the office adjoining his home room to make a phone call—she knew it would be the police next. She heard him speak and understood the notes of anxiety and confusion. She pocketed the banana and the biscuits and opened the station-house window and climbed outside and landed in a flower pot. She put her feet to the ground and quickly she was across the car park and over a fence and into the sidings and into the fields.

February.

The fields were cold and soft and wet as she crossed them and open to the skies and the wetness came through her trainers and a sharp wind cut across the fields and through the fabric of the anorak and of the dress to her bones. She kept to the edges of the fields and moved in quick darts. She kept down when cars went past. She beat away the briars of the ditches that swayed with the wind and the branches were bare but with swollen buds that told soon a cold spring would come. Now the birds were everywhere garrulous. She was at home again in the country—the rough lanes were home, and the ditches were home, and she could walk for miles; her heart lightened. After a time the country rose into hills. She knew that she was strong. She went for another hour, and then longer, and ate the banana—she ate it under a tree of early blossom by a rough stone wall and as she sat there motionless in the wind but for her chewing a sweet black mouse crawled from beneath a crack in the rocks of the wall and lowered itself to the ground on a strand of yellowed grass that leaned and bent slowly with its weight and always in the future she would think of this place as the place of the mouse blossom tree. She moved on again. After a while she saw a small town rise to the north and knew to keep clear of it. She walked along a country lane by its old stone walls. She saw nobody. Sometimes a dog's bark came from far off hoarsely and it was always the same dog. Another town stood up to announce itself, and she kept clear of it, and there was a great swathe of woodland ahead, rising, and she knew at once that she would climb to this wood—she was drawn to it strongly. She climbed a lane made dark by trembling hedges on either side and the chill in this laneway was intense and made of more than the air—it was malevolent, a badness—and it hurried her step, and soon she was in the late-winter of the woods, at the quick fade of the February day, and it was strange but familiar, the path that led through and became rougher, and there was the scent of the needles of the pines that she trampled and the wind was distant as she became lost in the woods, it was such as the wind at the edges of a dream, and she felt now a presence among the trees.

She hurried to get through the woods but it was everywhere around her, as gripping as a cold sea, and a terror built and would not relent—she knew that she was being watched. She hummed against the fear and flicked her eyelids rapidly but she was in disarray now as she felt the presence and she began to run and the root of a tree took her ankle—she went down. She reeled inside and vaulted on a high white screech of pain. She was wretchedly in pain. She lay there crying and in great pain as his shadow moved across her. The broken hatched light of the woods became impoverished as the day ended and his face was made of haze and shadow.

Hush, he said.

He leaned down close to her and her heart popped

clear of its box and clear of the trees and she clenched her teeth and prayed hard that she might wake from the bad dream—she did not wake.

Ah look it, he said. No one's dead.

He placed lightly a hand on the broken ankle and she lurched again in pain.

No one's dead, he said. As we always say at times of abject fucken disaster.

He was old and had the look of the woods—he was a ferny, mossy, twisted old thing, and all of his roots and fibres spoke of years long and deep in the shadows and out of the light. He was a small bony creature but limber, and he lifted her from the ground, and she felt his odd energies and strength, and now she was not afraid at all.

Best thing to do with pain, he said, is ignore the ignorant fucker.

As he carried her through the woods the effort caused his breath to labour but only slightly even though she was almost as big as he was. They came to a sudden clearing in the woods—a trailer was kept neatly there on blocks.

Do you have the English? he said.

No, she said.

No is a good start, he said.

He set her down on the plastic crate that worked as a step to the trailer. He pointed at her ankle. The tops of the trees swayed in the wind and sang.

Is the pain bad, missy?

He winced to explain the pain he meant.

Yes, she said.

We are making progress, he said, in leaps and bounds.

She smiled to show the perfect white of her teeth. He laughed at the smile. He considered her. He displayed with a sweep of the hand and a formal bow the bleakness of the woods surrounding.

Fine spot you picked, he said. There being no place known to man nor beast of grimmer fucken aspect.

He opened the trailer door with a poke of the foot and reached for her and carried her inside.

The Ox Mountains you decided to land in? he said. Christ on a bike.

The pain came again in a nauseous swooping and he saw it in her and spoke quietly against it and it fell away. About her was a solitary man's cabin. It had great neatness. There were stacks upon stacks of old books. There must have been thousands of them that lined the walls and made of the trailer a cave of books.

Did you come through the town? he said.

He set her down on a low armchair and stoked a fire of sticks in a potbelly stove.

Town? he said, and he made steeples of his knuckles for rooftops.

No, she said.

The fire took again and its glow filled the small trailer's room.

As well not to have, he said. That place is gone maniacal.

He fetched some bandaging from a high shelf and wrapped tightly her ankle.

The fucken vulgarity of people, he said.

He placed a pot of water to boil on the hot plate of the stove.

Not that I'd be passing judgement, he said. But the auld glamourpusses down in that town? On the sun beds and gettin' blood changes?

There are women of sixty down in that place now, he

said, with lickable legs. And faith that wasn't always the case around here.

He snorted a dangerous laugh and tears came to his eyes that she saw were made of this mad mirth and she chuckled, too. The trailer held also a low table and a hard-backed chair and there was a pallet bed on the floor. She thought of her brothers far away. She knew that by now they would be crying for her, their tiny worlds cracked open to fear and confusion, and she echoed their cry—

Kizzy!

Is that your name? he said.

She nodded—she had the word.

Kizzy, he said, you are most certainly not vulgar.

He made her tea with leaves and settled to drink a cup with her.

I'd say we have serious trouble on our hands, Kizzy. But what's trouble today can seem like nothing tomorrow. Are you with me or agin me?

She smiled.

Good, he said. We'll make a job of this calamity yet.

He took down a loaf of bread and a pot of jam and he

cut a thick slice and spread it with butter and the jam and it was the finest thing she had eaten ever.

Would you believe the jam is made by my own fair hand? he said. If I'm nothing else I'm knacky.

She found somehow the belief that her brothers would know she was all right, that she was strong, and that she was guided in the world. She did not care what her mother thought or believed.

We'll figure this out between us, Kizzy, the old man said.

THAT FIRST NIGHT she slept hardly at all—it was not out of fear but out of strange excitement. She lay on the pallet bed as he lay on the floor and she listened to his breathing and tried to decide if it was a type of elf that lay there—it could not be an elf for this was not a dream—and the sound of the high wood by night in the wind was all about them and it was as real as the slow pumping inside that was the motion of her settling heart.

KIZZY?

She had slept at last for a while but she woke to the word again, and there was more tea to be had, and it rained hard on the roof of the trailer.

A day for the books, he said.

He was busily all the morning about his books. He hunted through old volumes. He made tsssking sounds and gasps of affirmation.

Right so, he said, reading.

Kizzy, he said, is the Romani form of the Hebrew Qetsiyah, which is a bark similar to cinnamon.

A flavoursome young lady, he said, that's named for the fucken trees.

HE WAS NO ELF but simply a tiny old man. His contact with the towns and villages beyond the woodland was minimal. Sometimes he sold wooden ornaments for

Christmas and net sacks of kindling at the car boot sales, and once a week he walked the miles to a twenty-four-hour supermarket at the edge of one of the bigger towns but he did so in the middle of the night when he knew the aisles there would be empty as desolation.

When it rained they stayed in with the books.

Her ankle soon mended.

When the bright spring days came they were about the woods and the mountain fields at the peripheries of the woods, as the wild garlic rose, and the blossom that formed on the bushes and hedges was an itch on the air and caused giddiness in them both. The understanding that grew between them was first of tone and gesture, and then of words, as she took them one by one and in compounds from him, by the phrase and the sentence, and she took the colours of his dialect, and her own talk by tiny degrees took on the precise timbre of his, just as her own young malleable life took on the form of his—they settled to a type of collusion with each other. The pretence that they must puzzle out their dilemma was soon dropped. It became clear that this was where she wanted to be. There were no questions to be answered here. None except for the simple questions of when to eat and when to sleep and when to work, and slowly, the dilemma was allowed to disappear and was replaced by the quiet efficiencies of love, and both knew that she had come to the end of her path, and she would go no further.

He gave her his life. He gave her the routines and tiny errands of it. The basic skills that were needed for the making of Christmas ornaments, and the ways of the wheedling at the car boot sales, and he taught her that always a distance should be maintained, that there need be no others. He taught her the rituals of the year in this damp and temperate place. She grew to young womanhood in the hatchlight of the woods and its sudden clearances. After her first menstrual cycle, a second trailer was bought and placed beside his. He kept her by a native canniness from the prying of officialdom. As time passed they would go for days and weeks often without speaking to each other—there wasn't the need for it. She lived long and calmly, and calmly even went the moment of his eclipsing, when she became and replaced him, and laid her fingertips on his eyelids to close them, and she took on the forces of the place, as he had granted them to her, and she could vanish at will into the dark cool recesses of the woods.

THERE WERE TIMES of great change beyond the woods, but it did not matter, and the noises of the towns sometimes grew frantic—it did not matter; she read her books—and there were times of mobbed voices and great migrations—it did not matter—and there was the time of the fires across the lakes—it did not matter—and the gaseous blue of their after-glare, but all of it soon faded again and passed, and did not matter.

EVEN YET the woodland each year stretches out and grows, like the shadow of a disease spreading, and soon the century will turn again, and her trailer's flue will for just a little while longer twist its penlines of ash smoke through the hatching of the trees, and when she speaks to herself, on these final days, it is in the accent of the place, of the Ox Mountains. If there is a sadness it is that her brothers have long since disappeared—first their faces went, then their voices—and she can recall them now only as an aggregate—the four black buttony heads, bopping, as playful as a sack of pups, and as vulnerable—but in truth she does not think of them that often.

EXTREMADURA (UNTIL NIGHT FALLS)

THE OLD DOG is tied by a length of rope to a chain-link fence. Its hackles comb up a silent growl as I approach through the edges of the small white town and its eyes burn a high yellow like witch hazel oddly vivid in such a skinny and unkempt old dog. A dog that has known some weather, I'd say. There are no people anywhere to be seen—I am in the last slow mile after dusk and my calves are singing. There is a café up ahead but it is shuttered and dark. I have walked for many hours and miles and in fact for almost fifteen years now. The dog eases into itself again as I come nearer and its flanks relax to this softer breathing and I crouch on my own hind legs by its side to converse for a while among the lights of our eyes.

It's as if I've known you for a long time, she says.

But when I lay my hand to her there is a shiver of nerves again as if she has known the cruelties, too. The town is not entirely quiet. Somewhere behind shutters there is the sound of a soccer game on the radio or TV. I used to be afraid of the dogs but they got used to me. Ever the more so as I walk I take on the colours and notes of the places through which I walk and I am no longer a surprise to these places. My once reddish hair has turned a kind of old-man's green tinge with the years and this is more of it. What the ramifications have been for my stomach you're as well not to know. I have very little of the language, even after all this time, but the solution to this is straightforward—I don't talk to people. This arrangement I have found satisfactory enough, as does the rest of humanity, apparently, or what's to be met of it in the clear blue mornings, in the endless afternoons.

We are coming out of a very cold winter in Extremadura, which is a place of witches, or at least of stories about witches. To be passing the nights, I suppose.

The dog has a good part of an Alsatian in her and random bits of mutt and sheepdog and wolf probably and she tells me of a thin life and a harsh one in this cold-hearted, in this love-starved town.

Go on? I says.

The lamps above us catch and buzz for a moment as their circuits warm and also to mark the sombre hour there is the hollow doom of the church bells—they lay it on heavily enough around these places still.

Footsteps, now, as the bells fade out to echoes, and there is a girl of about sixteen years old and she does not see me at all but mouths the words of a popular song, a song that is current, I believe it is a Gaga, I know it well enough myself from the cafés and the concourses—all the years I have doled out in that same old (it seems to me) estación de autobuses that exists at the edge of all these towns; I use them not for the buses but for sleeping—and she moves swaying down the road in a cloud of distraction (if *sleep* is what you could call it!) and she hums as she goes and she is not a pretty girl exactly but neither plain and what she has in truth is a very beautiful carriage—buenas tardes?

She turns in surprise over her shoulder but there is not a glimmer, really, she just blinks and moves on, and the dog simpers and stretches; now there is the chug of a moto as it troubles its lungs to mount a rise in the road and a shutter is pulled inwards on a hard sharp creak and the sound of the soccer game loudens; all across the silver hills in the east the cold spring night lovelessly descends. February is an awful fucking month just about everywhere. The waft of sweet paprika and burnt garlic from a kitchen somewhere. Still there is no life at the café. Whatever is going on with that place. Far away in the north my very old parents must be waiting for me or for word of me, at least; they are waiting for me still at the bottom of the dripping boreen framed by the witchy haw and the whitethorn. It's what keeps them going, I'd say.

I don't know what people take me for as I pass along the edges of the roads. What money I have is by now so comically eked out and in such tiny dribs that my clothes are not good at all and as certain as the weeping callouses on the balls of my feet is the need for new boots or a pair of good trainers. I sleep generally where I fall. In doorways sometimes, or if the weather's foul in the cheapest hostels run always by spidery old women in black, or in the bus concourses, under the benches, or in the lee of buildings, or on the black sand beaches in the south if the winter is especially long and hard and I've took a turn down the road for myself. At one time *southerned* was a very common word and southerning a practice. For the better of the lungs and so forth. Sometimes I'm not sure what century I've mistaken this one for and I wonder would I be better off elsewhere and in other times. Sometimes I feel as if my engines are powered on nothing at all but the light of the pale stars that will emerge above us now. I can get by on almost nothing and it is conceivable that I might become very, very old myself, and as spidery. The summers don't present much of a problem. You can always find cool places.

The moto comes into the line of our vision, its engine turns off for the decline of the road, and it coasts, and a teenage boy steers and parks it beneath a tree across the way from me. He steps off and looks over and nods and lights a cigarette and he looks down along the road after the singing girl and she senses his glance and turns a look back to him—her thick black hair moves—and their eyes catch for a moment but as quickly she turns from him and is gone; an old man appears as though from the dust and sits on a half-collapsed bench by a white wall that it seems clear to me was at one time bullet-riddled. Now we all watch each other closely and the sense of this is companionable enough. A heavy-set middle-aged man appears in just a flimsy yellow t-shirt that reads *Telefonica Movistar*—suddenly it's all go—and he crosses the road to the boy with the moto—he mustn't feel the cold—and he talks to him and they look down calmly together at the workings of the bike, each of them with their hands on their hips and their cigarettes at a loose dangle from their mouths, and they squint through the smoke at the little moto and its failing organs and the man reaches for it, turns the key, revs it, listens with his head inclined at an expert's careful angle, and lets it die again and shakes his head. Not long for the road by the looks of things.

I crouch on my hind legs with the dog whose snout rests in the curve of my shoulder now and she whispers to me that the girl is named Mercedes and is wanted by not a few of the young louts around this place with big rough hands on them—these are country people—and she has already in fact given it to one or two of them. On Saturdays. The clocks must have stopped for them. But awful to be sixteen or eighteen and already your finest hour has gambolled past like a grinning lamb and your moto is fucked also.

Now the sky makes a lurid note of the day's ending—there are hot flushes of pink and vermilion that would shame a cardinal. The chain-link fence encases nothing but a crooked rectangle of dirt and dead tyres and stones—old chicken ground maybe—and it has an air of trapped misery.

And more than that you're as well not to know, the dog says.

Dogs, I find, are much the same everywhere. Much of a muchness, as my father would say. They know everything about us and love us all the same. My father when he wanted the sound of the television up or down he would say highern it or lowern it. One time in Ronda I nearly fucked myself into the gorge there altogether. A thousand-foot fall would have settled the question decisively. But I thought that might be a bit loud. I am not by nature a man who has that kind of show in him. No extravagances.

The old man calls across to the pair by the moto. It is a weak scratchy call like an injured bird would make. The pair by the moto ignore him utterly. Another shutter opens. A TV bleats a game show's jingle. The sky pales again as quickly as it coloured. As if somebody has had a Jesuitical word. That ours beneath this vaulted roof might be an austere church. There was a time when I tried to fill the sky with words. Morning and fucking night I was at it. In my innocence, or arrogance—the idea that I might succeed. But I walked out of that life and entered this one.

The teenage boy kicks the back wheel of the fucked moto; the middle-aged man in the t-shirt laughs to make his belly rise and fall. A hunting bird moves across the acres of the sky in the last thin light of day and a breeze comes up the road with quick news—a tree shakes out its bare branches and moves. There is a twist of rancid olive oil on the air over the odour of stale dog. I'm sorry but there is no pretty way to say it. I wonder if I was to make off with you altogether? I could slip this rope from you as easy as anything.

I'd love to go, she says, and yet I'd not go. Do you know that kind of way?

Oh but I do. I'd love to go home again but I will not go. Imagine? Coming up the boreen in County Roscommon with my tale of the lost years and my rucksack of woes and the little gaunt tragic sunburnt face on me? Wouldn't they love to see it coming? I do believe they're back there still—I believe they're alive and that I'd know somehow if they weren't.

I stepped onto a train that night in Madrid and out of my life.

Love?

Don't mention it.

They must whisper their love to Mercedes as night falls. A hand cupped neatly to the shape of her groin. The question mark of it. The old man gets up from the bench and walks like a clockwork scarecrow by the side of the road. I stand again to stretch out my bones. If I looked hard enough, I'd find a café open someplace among these white-walled streets and hidden turns—I could have coffee with hot milk. But I have nearly had my fill of the cafés. There is only so much of that business you can take. And there is the danger always of the cerveza and the brandy. There are only so many times you can climb over that wall.

I rise onto the tips of my toes and look along the darkening sky and road and here she comes again, Mercedes, and still she jaws vaguely on her song—buenas tardes?

But again she ignores me and it is as if she cannot see me even. She carries beneath her arm a carton of table wine—*tinto* is one of the words I have, and never too far from the tip of my tongue—and a jar of Nutella and in a blue plastic bag a frozen octopus. This will mean a grocer open down the road someplace with a stick of bread for me. Tentacles and spindles and bulbous sacs—I need to dig into myself harder lately for the words of things.

The dog is up beside me and she sniffs at the air after Mercedes and the evening falls away from us quickly. I'll need to decide soon where to lie down tonight. The animal must choose its lair. The first stars burn coldly on the plain and I am so many miles from home.

I reach out for you a last time. Your warm skinny flank

and the way that you sigh and move closer to me just once more just this one last time. I slip a finger under the rough collar of rope and work to loosen it and you settle in this moment that much closer to me.

A moto runs its troubled lungs; the young girl's step recedes; the old man's falters.

The man in the yellow t-shirt passes along and he says hello to the dog and he looks right through me. This is no place for me tonight, I decide—I would rather not their shelter. I'll move on again and maybe tonight I'll keep moving all the way through until the sunlight wakes the yellow of the fields of rapeseed and in truth I am still drinking some of the time because I have not yet drank her all the way out of my mind and I still have this broken heart.

THAT OLD COUNTRY MUSIC

HANNAH CRYAN waited in the Transit van up in the Curlews. Setanta Bromell had parked so that the van was secreted in the shade of the Forestry pines and could not easily be seen from the road. He had taken the dirtbike from the back of the van then and headed down to Castlebaldwin pissing smoke. His morning's ambition was to rob the petrol station there with a claw hammer. Setanta was her fiancé of these recent times and, despite it all, the word still rolled glamorously to her lips.

It was the second Monday of May. She was a little more than four months pregnant. The whitethorn blossom was decked over the high fields as if for the staging of a witch's wedding. Already the morning was humid and warm, and snaps of wind cut from the hillsides and sent the blossom everywhere in vague, drifting clouds. Even with the windows shut, her eyes streamed, and she could feel sore pulses in her throat like slow, angry worms. Setanta was thirty-two years old to her seventeen and it was not long at all since he had been her mother's fiancé.

That's the way it goes sometimes with close-knit families, he said.

Don't even fucken joke about it, she said.

Setanta's plan—if it could be held up to the light as such—was to get into the petrol station just after it opened, show the claw hammer, and start roaring out of himself. As she waited on the mountain, Hannah jawed helplessly on her gums and tapped her phone for the time—it showed 7:17 a.m. and then died.

Fuckwad, she said, and threw the phone to the dash.

Castlebaldwin was a ten-minute scramble away and he'd been gone for more than twice that. The van had laboured to climb even the low mountains of the Curlews and she tried not to think deeply about its viability for escape. The drone from the N4 down below was becoming more steady, the morning traffic thickening to a stream. It was difficult to believe that just last night she had laughed with excitement as she took the first baby bump photo for her Insta and Setanta's needle buzzed jauntily as he tattooed a lizard on his left calf. He told her in a voice scratchy with emotion that he loved her and that their souls were made of the same kind of stuff. She licked his earlobe and showed him the selfie and he cried in hard, gulpy jags. She did not remark that the lizard looked more like it had frog dimensions, really, nor that the rapid blinking effect had returned to Setanta's left eye.

She had asked him to leave the keys of the van but he would not. When he had a plan worked out his mouth fixed into a tight hard rim like a steel toecap. In truth, she knew well that Setanta Bromell of Frenchpark was not making solid decisions lately. She sneezed and reflexively laid a hand to her belly to reassure the visitor. High slants of sunlight now breached the top of the Forestry pines and showed a stretch of scarred hillside rising to Aghanagh bog. The gorse on the higher hills was lit from the inside out an electric living yellow. Dead for half a year the Curlews were like some casual miracle reviving. Setanta Bromell said that May, always, was the number one month of the year for going mad.

Passing through the narrow kitchen of her mother's house, four and a half months previously, he had placed a hand to her skinny hip and turned on the cow eyes and that was enough. Her mother when she'd been drinking slept like the dead. By night, it had become the custom that Setanta and Hannah would talk. She liked to listen to his stories about work. He told her about the man with the huge swastika on his back that Setanta had remodelled into the ancient flag that showed in quadrants the symbols of the four proud provinces of Ireland: the red hand, the triple crown, the hawk and dagger, the harp.

Better a 'Ra head than a Nazi, he said.

There was a quick russety shimmer through the yellow gorse as a fox moved for her den. Hannah's lips moved softly at the sight and made a wordless murmuring. Now the birds were going dipshit unseen in the hedges, in the pines. Setanta Bromell owed her mother, like, four grand? His eyes rolled up as if to see the stars when he came.

She waited. The Transit van smelled like a stale morning mouth. She listened for the growls of the dirtbike climbing the backroad but no sound rose above the birds, above the N4's sea-like drone, above the hot wind in gusty snaps from the hillside.

Her hands lay folded loosely across her belly. She tried to do what the lady doctor at the clinic had told her to do in the panic times—she felt out her breaths on an individual basis. You had to get yourself on intimate terms with every breath that passed through your body. You had to listen to each breath as it travelled and smooth out its journey. In the Transit she sat and concentrated as well as she could but still her breaths came short and wildly.

Now the sunlight broke fully across the canopy of pines and came starkly through the van. Hannah closed her eyes against it to see dreamy pink fields on the backs of her lids. She clawed at the greasy vinyl of the seat. She listened, and in the gaps between the wind it was just the birds in conference, in the high springtime excitedly, a vast and unpredictable family.

Still on the air there was not a whisper of Setanta Bromell's dirtbike.

He did not drink much. She'd say that for him. He would sit up late while her mother slept. For a long while, they had sat at opposite ends of the L-shaped sofa, as far apart from each other as they could get, which in itself had signalled a situation. He said that particular stretches of ground had for him a lucky vibration. He said the Curlews most of all. Once a prime buck had skittered from the ditch and lurched into the side of the van and dropped stone dead of the shock and all Setanta had to do was haul it home and hang it to be skinned.

These are the type days I get in the Curlews all the time, he said.

He spoke often of fatedness and of meant-to-be's. Then came the three a.m. of his soft, slow hand in the kitchen, and it was a case of smoochy-smoochy and throwing each other up against the walls before anyone knew the fuck what was going on.

She pulled down the sun visor for its mirror. She had a face on her like a scorched budgie. She detested her new self. By nature like a stick, she was taking on weight with the pregnancy. Beneath her breath, she made the words of a Taylor Swift song for distraction but the song did not take.

News headline: there was no sign of Setanta Bromell on no fucking dirtbike.

She saw him with his limbs splayed on the petrol station floor. She heard the ratchety cruel tightening of the cuffs. Or maybe the Belarusian who worked the morning shift had just hopped the counter and grabbed the hammer and laid Setanta out flat with a single bop to the broadside of the head. The Belarusian was a massive fuck who must have weighed about as much as a cement mixer. Setanta's plan had gaps and weak spots.

Hannah Cryan climbed from the van and walked from the Forestry pines onto the backroad. By now the morning had clouded over and the vast spread of the whitethorn blossom across the hillsides and the high fields and the ditches made an ominous aura as it moved in the wind. Once, as a child, she had been slapped across the face by her mother for bringing an armful of the blossom into the house. The whitethorn flowers so much as passing the threshold was a harbinger of certain death in the family. By about the Tuesday of the next week. She had meant it as a gift for her lovely young mother.

As she sat on a five-bar gate up in the Curlew Mountains the great meanness of the morning descended on her. She hummed a string of four or five notes against the meanness, not knowing where they came from nor how.

The plan was that they would drive through the day and the north to the ferry at Larne for Stranraer, and from there descend through Scotland and the Borders—she watched his lips move as he recited solemnly the steps of it—through Cumbria to Yorkshire and to his cousins in the city of Wakefield. Over the nights, as they conspired, the word "Wakefield" had taken on the burnish of legend. She saw the city lights spread out. She imagined a child with a north of England accent and a neat little flat in a tower block. She saw herself and Setanta in the bed eating toast and taking photos of each other—his muscles flexed; her eyelashes fitted—and the toddler gurgling along in pure happiness on the rug on the floor. Setanta Bromell might soften his cough in Wakefield, she believed, and think harder about his decisions, and forget all the nonsense with the lizards and the claw hammers.

The day was up and about itself.

The fields trembled.

Catastrophe was a low-slung animal creeping darkly over the ditches, across the hills.

Her mother had found her one careless morning under the throw on the sofa, topless and asleep in the hot, emotional clutches of Setanta Bromell. That had made it a morning for the annals. Since then, they had slept in two sleeping bags zipped together at his King Ink studio. The studio was located over a butcher's shop in Boyle. It reeked of their wild love and animal death. Setanta was eighteen months behind on the rent and had a notice to quit and lately this involuntary blinking in the left eye.

But desperate times, he said, very often turned out to be disguised opportunities.

Wakefield, as a shimmering prospect, was held aloft before her like a priest's chalice.

By now she knew that he would not come back from Castlebaldwin. On the five-bar gate of a tiny farm high in the Curlew Mountains she again closed her eyes for the pink fields. She went into a dream. If the moment was never-ending it might not even exist. She felt the presence of something very old and uncaring on the air. An insect's steady keening from the ditch was incessant like a hopeless prayer or the workings of his needle. He had tattooed on her inner thigh a swallow in flight.

In the black times make you think of summer, he said.

In the black times, she thought, it'd take more than a badly drawn swallow aiming for my fucken gash.

He was probably in the holding cell at Ballymote already. He was already on first-name terms with every guard in the vicinity. Setanta Bromell was—and here the words came unbidden, as if from an old ballad recalled—already in chains. The new life within twitched with nervous expectancy. As if it knew already of all the disasters to come.

Hannah Cryan came to ascend from herself. Above the green fields and the whitethorn blossom moving in the morning wind, above the stone walls and the Forestry pines, above the inland sea of the grasses, above the broken drone of the motorway, above all of this she measured out the stretch of her seventeen years. They had been mean and slow-feeling years. She was almost as old as the century and felt it. Her man in jail and a child at the breast—it was all playing out by the chorus and verse.

Her legs weak, her step uncertain, feeling lightheaded and frightful, she trailed back to the van and climbed into it. She sucked the last warm dregs from a bottle of water on the dash but her thirst was not sated. Often he kept six-packs of sparkling water from Aldi in back of the van. For his digestion, he said, which was at the best of times troublesome.

She got out and opened the back doors and rooted around among her fiancé's astonishing detritus. She found no water but she did find the ten-euro claw hammer from Simons Brothers hardware.

The scales of the morning fell away.

She stood by the side of the van with the claw in her hand.

She swung it hard and precisely to extract the eyes from the brute, lying face of Setanta Bromell. That the sockets might dangle and his lively tongue loll.

She hadn't the strength to climb back in the van. She sat on the ground on the pine kernels and cried for a short while. A few months ago she had been skin and flint and edges and points—she had been hard—but now she was softened and plush like a lazy old cat. It was foreign to her. She felt slowed and mawkish with it. He had softened her merely with glances, his touch and words. More than softened, she had been opened.

On the mountain time loosened, unspooled.

The fields blinked.

The gorse whispered.

Morning?

It must have been coming by now for noon. If she had the legs to carry her, they might take her the five miles down to Boyle. But if she did not get past this moment, she would not have to face the next.

She looked out across the high fields. Just now as the cloudbank shifted to let the sun break through the whitethorn blossom was tipping; the strange vibrancy of its bloom would not tomorrow be so ghostly nor at the same time so vivid; by tacit agreement with our mountain the year already was turning. The strongest impulse she had was not towards love but towards that burning loneliness, and she knew by nature the tune's circle and turn—it's the way the wound wants the knife wants the wound wants the knife.

Now she heard before its sound even broke on the air the scratch and meek resolve of her mother's Corolla. It was neither taxed nor insured. It was taken out only at moments of high emergency. These were not yet so few as her poor mother might have hoped.

And yes, here it came, inevitably, around the bend from the backroad into the Forestry pines, and Hannah felt a volley of tiny kicks within.

Lou-Lou Cryan was a hollowed woman now. She was like a reed from the drink and the nerves. She stepped from the Corolla and came soft-footed and stoically through the gloom of the pine trees to take her daughter in her arms.

Oh you poor fool, she said. Oh you poor sweet fucking fool.

ROETHKE IN THE BUGHOUSE

In 1960, the American poet Theodore Roethke and his wife Beatrice spent time on the island of Inishbofin, off the coast of County Galway. While on the island, Roethke had a breakdown and was committed to the psychiatric hospital at Ballinasloe, back on the mainland.

THE LIMBS of a dead whitethorn appear in the dark to say that the night dissolves. The large dishevelled man fills the hospital window with a spidery grin as the last of the dark gives out to grey morning. The morning comes up after a night such as this and you feel like you've fought a fucking war. Now come the slate roofs and the chimney pots and all the weary rest of it—Ballinasloe is greyly waking. He turns to the slight man sat neatly in a bedside chair with palms rested on cheerful knees.

—What did you say your name was, Doctor?

—I didn't. I'm O'Reilly.

—Oh, I'd believe it.

The doctor has spatters of mud or cowshit on the hems of his trousers. Equine snout, tiny head. He half rises from the chair and turns it to face the thin new light in the window and sits again.

—And how should I address you, Mr. . . .

—It's Ret-kuh. But you can call me Ted.

This all seems entirely reasonable. Yes I am Ted and I am made of flesh, bones and gases, and this spidery grin. Anxiety folds away its arbitrary music. Unquestionably I could use a drink also. Now the large man can feel the grin detach itself from the tight lines of his mouth. August here is dense as a jungle in the rain and it plays sour notes in his glands and pulses.

—Are you experiencing agitation, Ted?

—Well!

All this and heaven, too. He arranges a sigh and to emphasise it rests a buttock on the edge of the mattress. Bony as an army bed. The doctor crosses his legs now.

The doctor sits a kind, interested chin on his knitted fingers.

—In truth, Dr. O'Reilly, I'd say there's been nothing that's absotively a surprise to me.

All this coming and going from himself. He would like very much now to spread his fat limbs in the water. Because I could float like a lilypad and I am beautiful in the water, I have such grace when I am floating there. There is a burning sensation in his chest. He would like a tall stiff drink and he would like to fumble with some skirt in a taxi. I think I could make you shriek, actually.

—What it is, it's a fucking joke, you take absolutely and positively and stick 'em together, I am aware of my fucking words, O'Reilly.

What is it, the line from Hopkins? I am gall, I am heartburn. You need to try some Pepto-Bismol, friend, and you need to try it today. This doctor's head is quite simply too small for a grown man's, it gives him a beany look. Very punchable.

—I understand that you write?

—Oh, angelically.

On Inishbofin he looked to the sky and saw fires on the moon. He lay wrapped in his overcoat on the pier all night long and for a while a safe harbour it seemed. Yes there was a bottle and Mars also was visible.

—About this recent unpleasantness, Doctor. It's nothing I can't handle.

Cold white wine. A bellyful of shellfish. A hotsy-totsy in a yellow cab. The city's rank night odours. Her pearl buttons straining. And seeing as you ask, girl? Well yes, the thought is always crossing my mind. And I do mean always. I think that we could do filthy things together. Just you and me.

—I believe that it's poetry, Ted?

—Fuck off.

—Ah now.

—I'm sorry.

—That's all right. I believe it's poetry that you write?

So do I—no, that's pat, the line swings out too easily.

—It intends to be.

Oh you pompous ass with your handsome jowls, your lurching heart! This doctor is a religious, I can tell, the placid godhaunts of his pale green eyes.

—Did you come loose of yourself on Bofin, Ted?

—That's a very attractive way of putting it, Doctor.

Here we are in our sombre grey palace. Here we are in our stone grey town. *Bal-in-a-sloe,* apparently. Sloe gin. Slow love. Shall we make an afternoon of it, lady? I watched you walk the beach on the island, Beatrice, and the breeze moved the sand in circling drifts, and it settled and sang again in the breezeless gaps, and you found in the white sand your ritual things, your pebbles and shells, and the way you dipped like a bird to peck them free.

—At the very least we can try some other medicines, Ted. You'll sleep anyhow, I'm sure of that.

This is all very fucking civilised. The day comes up hot and airlessly to fill the sour green ward and we connive most sensibly, this smiling doctor, this somewhat penitent loon. Though in truth I would quite like to fuzz up your smile, O'Reilly. See if you might misplace your faith. Shall I lead you through the caverns of this fat old skull then? Dank, oh dank places! Caverns full of black hissing water through which sometimes still I rise up to myself.

—You're crying a lot, Mr. Roethke.

—It's because I'm so tired now. The worst of this is done, believe me.

He had walked the corridors to pace off the night. He closed his eyes and drifted the island again as he paced. On Bofin there were bits of sheep everywhere. Hanks of dark bloodied wool along the roads and snagged in tidy clumps on the roadside wires. The road circled the island and brought him back to himself again. The road was so comically narrow he could lie across the entire breadth of it and did. He listened to the aches beneath the skin of the road. He conversed with the inanimate. Bloodied wool, rotted skulls, maggoty—there were horns and bones everywhere in neat piles cleaned smooth by the salt wind. Mutton necropolis. Lichen beautiful on the stones a yellowish green flecked with tiny black parts. I wonder if I exhaust you sometimes, dear Beatrice? It cannot be an easy ride. But of course I promise to write your name across the stars and years. That old promise. It is what sustains my kind. It is what keeps us coming in a grinning line. Ted Roethke walked the corridors almost the whole night through. Beyond the high windows the moon waxed heavily on County Galway.

—Did you know that madmen are much the same everywhere, Dr. O'Reilly?

—Much of a muchness, Ted, do you believe so?

—I do, actually.

Some whang-doodle off a hill farm—you can tell the hill people everywhere, too, the wind-startled look—some whang-doodle wept into his chest as he mooched the corridor and made two syllables again and again, a name, and wept to his chest, and I bet those were the syllables of his mama's name, her name forever on his dry cracked lips and his shit-crusted shirt-tail hanging all undone. What is with these Micks and their mothers? On Bofin grown men drank pints of milk with their spuds and stew. Creamy moustache, peat smoke, poem? Too easy, Ted. Fucking teat complex. Now ambition in the heavy morning jangles a single manic chord. He considers suavely the needle-thin doctor.

—Is this a reasonable kind of establishment, Doctor? Is this a reasonable kind of town?

—Tell me what you mean.

—Might a man go for his walk in the evenings, take the evening air?

—There's one pub I'll allow you to go to, Ted. Our nurses drink there and they'll look after you.

We understand each other, clearly. Yes, much of a muchness. I am the large trembling electrified type hot-eyed with unnameable passions. He has seen my cut so many times. Ted is smiling now, Ted is benevolent—he shifts the second buttock onto the mattress. The doctor murmurs encouragingly—a wood pigeon sound from his hollows, gently. Ted is moving in for a while. He will rest his bones here for a good long while. Certain concessions have been made. Hoarsely now a crow calls—the crows patrol the grounds in knee-high boots like swaggering swing-keys of the place.

—How have the nights been for you, Ted?

—The nights have been complicated.

—As though they might go on forever?

And full of occult music. The nights on Bofin were lit by the moon that lived above the harbour and yes, truly, there were fires on the moon. He sat on the pier and wrapped himself tightly in his overcoat. The wind moved in cold sharp points and ambition was again his currency.

Shall I never be satisfied, he asked himself, quite harshly, on the pier at Inishbofin, his legs crossed at the ankles.

—Is this a happy town or a saddish kind of town, O'Reilly?

—Do you believe that towns have their own emotions?

—It's clear to me. Also they are sexed.

—I'm interested in this.

—All you have to do is look out the fucking window, Doctor. This Ballinasloe is very obviously a female place.

He is priapic. He is humid. He is ambitious. If there was no ambition, he would not write at all. When it is so insistent—so flagrant, so grabby—it poisons every word that he writes. He can see the words queering on the page. And he sweats in the night and even as he drinks and even as he makes love, what he thinks is this: maybe I can make my own mythology still. Maybe it is ambition that can trace my name across the skies and years. And you will commemorate me then with greenéd brass plaques, in bars, and on piers—Theodore Roethke had a crack-up here.

—Would it apply to the countryside also, Ted? In

terms of places being sexed. What about the island, for example?

—The island I would say ambiguous.

On Bofin the baby rabbits tumbled white-assed from the ditches and scurried like our plans. The sheep were terribly fretful; the birds were so beautiful and played on the air. On the hospital corridor, in the night, an old man sat in a puddle of yellow piss and sang over and again a sentimental dirge:

—*I've been to a great many places, and wonderful sights I've seen, from Agernavoe to Ballinasloe . . .*

—And back to Ballyporeen. You have the air of it lovely, Ted. It's a Percy French song, though arguably not from his finest hour.

—I think everything is going to work out just fine between you and me, Dr. O'Reilly.

—We'll see how it goes. The most important thing is that there should be sleep.

—Oh, I agree, absolutely.

—The medicine will take hold of you and there will be sleep.

Take hold like a mother's arms. Well, that would

depend on the mother. The doctor rises and pleasantly retreats, this beany-headed soldier of reason. The large man puffs out his cheeks. The fields that he can see rising in the distance are lit now in a breakthrough sun, lit green like reason. This large, dishevelled but somehow still dapper man unties his laces and takes off his shoes. He somewhat casually loosens his tie, as if the workplace today was slightly difficult, darling, but no more than that. When you say you're going into work, as a writer, what you mean is you're about to crawl into your fucking nerves. He takes off his jacket and folds it away, careful as a boy. Soon there will be sleep and it will be a while then before I wake to my high, irreputable smile again. When I walked the cliffs on Bofin, yes, I was in an agitated climate. There were sudden recitals, blackouts, vitriol. I could see Theodore in the third person. The cliffs so pocked with rabbit holes, a rabbit metropolis, populous as Delhi. He uncapped the bottle as he walked the cliffs and the wind made eerie music in it—he swallowed the notes. They play inside him still in the caverns where the water is dark and hisses.

He lies down on his narrow hospital bed. He faces the

high, cracked ceiling that makes the vault for all these sweet-natured sobs and all these dark seethings. His mind runs now along a clean narrative strait and ambition once more is the motor—if such happens, then such will happen, and so on, all the way home on the heavenward line, and do you see now the way I can swing my jivey notes from all that happens?

Unkillable Roethke lies breathing and smiling in the sour hospital morning. Off Bofin the sea changed colour eight thousand times a day. Voices were held in tiny pockets inside the wind and travelled. His own words moved and came back to him and he could hear so clearly his lies and wheedling, he could hear his true and fervent love. He made notes incessantly even as he walked the hills and drank. The pages of the notebook filled up with his spidery scrawl. He grinned out the lines of it. And now from his bed in the morning in the hospital ward he calls out crossly:

—Oh! Can a man get some fucking sleep around here, please? Shut the fuck up you fucking loons or get the fuck out!

He has been to a great many places. He slaughtered a

dragon once on Second Avenue in Seattle. He battered some fiends in White Harlem. He has made some beautiful work, he believes—who the fuck is better than me? He has given himself a fucking shot at it, he believes. Because brokenheartedness is the note that sustains always and this he can play at will.

—Gentlemen! Quiet, please! I won't fucking ask you again!

By the time they get you in the bughouse, usually, the worst of it is over. His left hand rests on his fat belly to feel out each breath as it moves through his ribs and eases him. His right hand lies limply by his side but the index finger is busy and scratches quick patterns on the grey starched sheet—it makes words.

ABOUT THE AUTHOR

KEVIN BARRY is the author of the acclaimed novels *Night Boat to Tangier, Beatlebone,* and *City of Bohane* and the story collections *Dark Lies the Island* and *There Are Little Kingdoms.* His awards include the IMPAC Dublin Literary Award, the Goldsmiths Prize, the Sunday Times EFG Short Story Prize, and the Lannan Foundation Literary Award. His most recent book, *Night Boat to Tangier,* was longlisted for the Booker Prize and one of the *New York Times'* Best Books of 2019. His stories and essays appear in *The New Yorker, Granta,* and elsewhere. He also works as a playwright and screenwriter, and he lives in County Sligo, Ireland.

pare for TV appearances, and practice "impromptu" answers to reporters' questions. I had accompanied her across the country as she campaigned for her husband, and I wondered how she felt at this moment. Was she simply resigned, as I was, to her husband's defeat? Was she sad? Or perhaps, I thought, she was relieved—even glad—that at last it was over. Ted would, of course, return to the Senate. But what part would Joan play in his life now? What was in her future?

Below, the Garden overflowed with journalists, network technicians, and delegates who had come to hear Kennedy's address. He was seated on the stage, his family nearby. From the balcony, I could just make out Joan's blond hair glistening under the bright lights of the convention hall. Next to her sat her lovely twenty-year-old daughter Kara, a student at Trinity College, her hair long and brown. Beside her Teddy, Jr., nineteen and a student at Wesleyan, stockily built like his father, with a head of blond curly hair. On the other side of his mother, Patrick, thirteen, who attended school in Washington and watched everything with expressive brown eyes. And seated in rows near the stage, the rest of the Kennedys: sisters and brothers-in-law and their children, together as always like a brick wall in moments of family victory or defeat.

Finally, the Senator rose, and as he walked to the podium the assembled delegates felt a sudden charge of exhilaration. His supporters in blue and white hats waved blue and white signs; blue balloons floated into the air. Even those who had opposed him joined the tumultuous ovation. The last Kennedy of his generation, a dynamic figure in a dark suit, looked out over the hall and the crowd fell silent. He began to speak, and almost immediately he enveloped his audience with the energy of his delivery and the conviction of his message.

It was a dramatic and eloquent speech—a thirty-two-minute oration considered by many to be the greatest of Kennedy's political career. As the conscience of the Democratic party, the Senator reaffirmed in the familiar Kennedy accent that theirs was the party that cared about "the common man—and the common woman." Typical of his famous family's dedication to public service, he had worked tirelessly for his causes these past few months and now

1 DREAMS

It's a wonder I'm not drinking. Any other lady alcoholic going to a national convention where her husband could be nominated for President might drink. . . . We all know Ted might not get it, but what if he does? Oh, my God!

—JOAN

On the sidewalks outside New York City's Madison Square Garden, hawkers were busy pushing their wares: campaign pennants and buttons, and yellow and blue T-shirts with the motto "I Survived the 1980 Democratic National Convention." Inside, that night, supporters and delegates waited in anticipation for Senator Edward M. Kennedy to address the convention. Organ music swelled and receded, orchestrating the waves of Kennedy and Carter campaign hats, posters, and placards, bobbing in continual motion on the convention floor.

Sitting high in the balcony with other Kennedy staffers, overlooking that colorful scene, I sensed the impending drama and tried to accept the fact that our campaign was drawing to a close. The Senator's presidential aspirations had *not* survived the convention, and after he lost a crucial rules vote the night before, his valiant fight was over. Jimmy Carter's nomination was now inevitable, and in a moving statement to his staff, Kennedy had announced that he would withdraw from the race. He would not be a candidate for President of the United States.

For Joan Kennedy, too, the last few days had been a whirlwind of wooing delegates, meeting politicians and celebrities, and making appearances in the vast convention arena. As Joan's administrative assistant, I worked with her to review speeches, pre-

Finally, in recognition that hers has been an extraordinary life, this book is a tribute to Joan Kennedy. My hope that her story may prove to be valuable to others who face difficult choices in their own lives has made writing it a high point in my life, second only to having been a part of it.

princess to "poor Joan" to her final emergence as an independent woman. It was a story of love, marriage, and divorce, of what it was like to be a Kennedy, and of the deep conflicts between Joan's obligations as a political wife and her responsibility to herself. Yet as unique as her experiences were, there were also elements of Joan's life that mirrored the experiences of every contemporary woman and the choices that every wife and mother must often make. As I wrote the book, it was that theme that guided my selection of which episodes to include. For 1980, the pivotal year in Joan's life, I have used my own notes and the journal I kept about her participation in the campaign. For the years before and after, I have relied for the most part on Joan's own recollections and remarks about her life, her marriage and divorce, and the Kennedy family. Scenes that illustrate the causes and consequences of her alcoholism, her struggle to change and the effects of her choices are at the heart of the book, along with scenes that portray the people important in her life. I have used pseudonyms and changed the professions and residences of two of those people: "Hazel" and "Gordon." And in painting this portrait of Joan, I have tried to be sensitive, yet at the same time to write with honesty and insight in my belief that the greatest respect one can show another person is the attempt to understand.

Many people contributed generously to this work. I would like to thank Pamela Painter, who helped shape the book and advised me along the way; Kate Connell, who did the picture research; and Burton Beals, who edited the manuscript. I would also like to thank Diane Haynes, Dr. Merle Jordon of the Boston University School of Theology, John H. Livens, Carol Ann Paresky, Powers Answering Service, Helen Rees, Rev. David A. Works of the North Conway Institute, and William Wright for providing encouragement, editorial suggestions, or a quiet place to write. To my children, Dana and Brad, who patiently accepted my frequent unavailability while working for Joan and then while working on this book—my love. And to many friends and colleagues who consistently supported me and understood my purpose—my thanks. Above all, my appreciation goes to Fred Hills and Simon and Schuster for sharing a vision.

Temple to meet Vice President Mondale in debate, the entire audience rose to its feet with applause and cheers. Although the campaign ended in defeat for Ted, it was a personal victory for Joan.

It was not, however, my original intention to write a book about Joan Kennedy. Motivated by my own experience with alcoholism, after completing my job for Joan, I resumed work on a book for women about alcoholism. My dream for such a book was twofold: to help those recovering from alcoholism to find acceptance, and those still suffering to be treated with understanding and consideration. Researching the book, I met an Episcopal clergyman who, in the nearly forty years of his recovery, had devoted himself to helping alcoholics. He suggested that a book about Joan's success, written by a sympathetic friend, would make a valuable contribution to others afflicted with the disease. Encouraged by his support and enthusiasm, I began to write this book.

Once my purpose for the book was clear, I asked Joan to be a part of it. While we were still working together, I had told her that I thought her story should be known. The idea had intrigued her, but now she chose not to participate. Only after consulting professionals and trusted friends, who urged me to work independently, did I decide to continue. I soon realized, however, that Joan's victory over alcoholism was only part of her story. A shy and sheltered Catholic-school girl, she had made a "Cinderella" marriage to the handsome youngest son of one of America's richest, most ambitious and politically powerful families. But far from moving toward the happy ending of that fairy tale, beneath its glamorous surface her life became a nightmare. Overwhelmed by the Kennedys, devastated by her husband's infidelities, plagued by her own sense of failure, she descended into the despair of alcoholism. Remarkably, Ted's decision to run for the presidency stopped her downward spiral. Confronted by this formidable challenge, not only did she stop drinking, she found new self-confidence and purpose in campaigning for her husband. Still, a happy ending eluded her. Ahead lay the traumatic divorce that would terminate a marriage of twenty-three years, and the difficult time of readjustment before she could begin a life on her own.

Joan's story, then, was extraordinary in its span from fairy-tale

PREFACE

When I first met Joan Kennedy in 1977, she was living alone in Boston, apart from her husband and three children, undergoing treatment for alcoholism. She was "poor Joan" to her family and friends, "poor Joan" to the public that read the never-ending flow of articles and books about the Kennedys. Even during her husband Ted's race for the 1980 Democratic nomination for President, she was "poor Joan" to many of the reporters who covered the campaign. But it was during that campaign that I—and countless others—came to realize that the "poor Joan" image no longer applied. This vulnerable, sensitive woman had great perseverance and strength. How else did she survive such a long succession of personal and family tragedies? How else win her battle against the dependence on alcohol that had enslaved her for years? How else endure the arduous demands, and the final disappointment, of the campaign itself? And in the months that followed, how else find the courage to end her unhappy marriage and seek a life and identity of her own?

Joan was well aware of the curiosity she generated as a member of the famous Kennedy family. She was less aware that her successful struggle to overcome alcoholism and her decision to live her life for herself had made a difference in the lives of others. As her friend and administrative assistant for more than five years, I saw the impact she had made in the hundreds of letters she received from all over the country. I saw it, too, in the way she was greeted wherever she went during the 1980 campaign. On the evening in Helena, Montana, when she walked up the long center aisle of the Shrine

CONTENTS

Preface 9

1 Dreams 13
2 Becoming a Kennedy 26
3 One Day at a Time 53
4 The Strategy Meeting 69
5 Two Announcements 88
6 Official Madness 101
7 Croissants and Compliments 115
8 January in Iowa 128
9 Declarations of Independence 142
10 Toward New Images 159
11 Crossroads 173
12 Pressing Incidents 183
13 Dark Passages 196
14 Choices 207
15 Starting Over 215
16 Going Forward 228

For Dana and Brad

Published by Simon and Schuster
A Division of Simon & Schuster, Inc.
Simon & Schuster Building
Rockefeller Center
1230 Avenue of the Americas
New York, New York 10020
SIMON AND SCHUSTER and colophon are
registered trademarks of Simon & Schuster, Inc.
Manufactured in the United States of America

10 9 8 7 6 5 4

Library of Congress Cataloging in Publication Data

Chellis, Marcia, 1940-
Living with the Kennedys.

1. Kennedy, Joan. 2. Kennedy, Edward Moore, 1932- . 3. Kennedy family. 4. Legislators' wives—United States—Biography. I. Title.
E840.8.K35C44 1985 973.92'092'4 [B] 85-8106
ISBN 0-671-50152-6

LIVING WITH THE KENNEDYS

Marcia Chellis